PENGUIN BC

REBIRTH

Jahnavi Barua is a writer based in Bengaluru. Her first book, *Next Door*, a collection of short fiction, was published by Penguin India in 2008 to wide critical acclaim. Her second, a novel, *Rebirth*, was published in 2010 and shortlisted for the Man Asian Literary Prize and the Commonwealth Book Prize. *Undertow*, published in 2020, is her third book. She was awarded the Charles Wallace Trust Fellowship for Creative Writing in 2006. Her books are on the syllabi of many universities and her short fiction has been widely anthologized.

PRAISE FOR *NEXT DOOR*

'Like the Brahmaputra, Jahnavi Barua's stories are rich, full and flow with ease, with sudden startling glimpses of turbulence under the placid surface. A powerful and confident voice'—Shashi Deshpande

'Filled with deft descriptions, wrenching surprises and a deep understanding of what it means to be human, this first collection by Jahnavi Barua is worthy of a careful read'—Chitra Banerjee Divakaruni

'Jahnavi Barua's stories are charged with affection for a landscape and an understanding of how it enters the human patterns of loving and living. A wonderful and moving book'—Anjum Hasan, author of *Lunatic in My Head*

'A striking debut that marks [Jahnavi Barua] as someone to watch'—Chandrahas Choudhury, author of *Arzee the Dwarf*

ALSO BY THE SAME AUTHOR

Next Door

Undertow

Rebirth

a novel

JAHNAVI BARUA

PENGUIN BOOKS

An imprint of Penguin Random House

PENGUIN BOOKS

USA | Canada | UK | Ireland | Australia
New Zealand | India | South Africa | China | Singapore

Penguin Books is part of the Penguin Random House group of companies
whose addresses can be found at global.penguinrandomhouse.com

Published by Penguin Random House India Pvt. Ltd
4th Floor, Capital Tower 1, MG Road,
Gurugram 122 002, Haryana, India

Penguin
Random House
India

First published by Penguin Books India 2010

ISBN 9780143414551

For sale in the Indian Subcontinent only

Typeset in Sabon MT by Eleven Arts
Printed at Repro India Limited

www.penguin.co.in

This is a legitimate digitally printed version of the book and therefore might not
have certain extra finishing on the cover.

For Arjun

The week your father left, in the beginning of July, four months ago now, I took to sitting in different places around the flat. Before that I had been partial to the large soft sofa in front of the television, from where I had a good view of the screen, but from where I also looked inwards, into the heart of the house. I did not see much of the sky or the buildings clustered around our own, but all that, anyway, did not cross my mind very often, so focused was I on your father and myself and the home we had fashioned together.

Sometimes—not very often—when I missed the open skies of my childhood, I would step out of the flat, locking it carefully behind me, and run up the stairs to the terrace where I was surrounded by the sky. Still, it was never as blue as I remembered and I was left with an ache in my stomach as I leaned against the low wall. A stiff wind was always blowing up there; that was the one thing that had marked Bangalore for me when we first came here, your father and I, seven years ago—the wind. The city of winds I had thought it then. I was a little afraid of the breeze as it pushed me against the parapet, belligerently, as if daring me to defy it. That and the thought that I was so visible there, laid open to the eyes of others in the buildings that encircled us and also, indeed, to those in our own always made me uneasy; I never stayed more than ten minutes before hurrying down to our flat again.

Since July, I have discovered many new things about my own home. From the low Rajasthani chair placed alongside the television, Ron's—your father's—favourite chair, I find I can see the sun rise in a long strip of sky fringed by coconut palms and the turreted tops of apartment buildings. Most of the time the sunrises are disappointingly bland—the deep blue of the early-morning sky simply lightens and clears until a pale light fills it—but every now and then, I am startled by an event full of drama, when swirls of hot colours, pinks, reds, oranges and peaches, accompany the flaming disc of the morning sun.

This was the time, earlier, when your father would be dashing around the house, getting ready for work, for the bus that took him to the software company's office, fifteen kilometres away, arrived promptly at seven o'clock. In the early mornings he was a demon, your father was, impatient and full of vitriol when anything went wrong. I was careful to lay out his clothes on the bed just as he liked to have them: clean underwear, vest and socks; then a crisp shirt and matching trousers; finally the belt. He was so particular about his clothes that I hand-washed them in Genteel myself and hung them, inside out, to dry on the clothes stand in the veranda that ran along the front of our flat. The veranda faced due west and by noon the sun blazed down on it uncaringly and I had to remember to bring in the clothes lest they fade. I even did all the ironing myself, meticulously placing a white linen cloth on the trousers so they would not get all shiny and look old before their time.

Once he was through with his bath and was dressed in his fresh clothes your father wanted a hot breakfast on the table. That really was no burden for I loved cooking; strangely—I should not be telling you this—but it made me feel desirable in a way I could not really account for. Was it the fact that I was feeding this man I loved food prepared with my own hands? Whatever it was, I adored sitting across from him watching him eat, slowly and carefully, his long, tapering fingers so sure as they went about their business. Your father looked so handsome in the mornings as he set off for work. They say men look best in formal attire—suits, jackets, ties— but even a work shirt and a pair of trousers with knife pleats is as good sometimes.

That had been the hardest time of all for me, the early mornings, in the beginning soon after he had gone. I missed the tense activity around the flat that had been part of my mornings ever since I had married your father. I could not bear to look at the dining table where we had sat together talking about all the small things that people married for a long time talk about: the bills to be paid, the impending bonus from office, the holiday we would take to Goa later in the year. I seldom ate with him so I did not mind eating alone but the emptiness of the mornings had closed over my head until I felt I was drowning. It is better now, although there are times I still wake up all hollow and weepy as if I have had a particularly sorrow-filled dream, but I have discovered, as I told you, new things that distract me, like the sunrise.

I have even ventured into the guest-room which looks out on to an abutting building and has no particular advantages; it is a cold, charmless room that no matter how much I endeavour—changing the linen, adding a bed-skirt to the bed, switching the furniture around—never feels warm. Maybe it is the lack of human presence in it that makes it so. I always felt a chill there as I walked in and even now see no appeal in it.

Your room—the third room—is another place altogether. Warm and sunny, it overlooks, on the northern side, a cluster of small bungalows with their multicoloured gardens, and a jacaranda, tall and feathery, is right outside the eastern window. It has always contained uncommon possibilities— your father and I often discussed how we would decorate it when you arrived; we squabbled, of course, your father being how he was, he wanted painted furniture while I had set my heart on pine—warm, knotty pine—and I made so many trips to the furnishing store on 100 Feet Road, where I fingered the blue chenilles, the velvets, the linen until I was too embarrassed to visit again.

You certainly took your time to show up. Year after year, we waited, your father and I, nerves jangling every time my period was late; but every time, like a leaky tap, I bled and wept but never gave up. I never gave up on you, I want you to know that. In the last year I sensed that your father had given up and I tried to tell him not to but he was already drifting away from me and nothing I said seemed to make a difference anymore.

It had all been too much for him, I think. The hospital trips, the endless tests, the injections, all those nights of tense couplings; in the end he just gave up. I went on planning though and even ventured out to a furniture factory on Sarjapur Road, as recently as in June, to look for a cot for you.

Stop being silly, Kaberi, your father had said, when I asked him if I could take the car and driver that morning, but he did not forbid me to go. So I went to the factory and there I found the cot I was looking for. It is waiting there for you now; last week I called the manager and placed an order. It will arrive as soon as I ask for it. December will be a good time to get it in—all the Christmas sales will be on and I will be able to pick up all the furnishings at good prices. There are the Diwali sales on now in October, but I am still feeling queasy in the mornings and, in any case, I have not told anyone yet and my friends will wonder if I have finally submitted to madness after all.

Coming back to your room. I now sit in it very often, especially in the late afternoons when I can hear a dove calling from the mango tree in the Raos' compound. The consoling gurgling of the bird takes me back home, to my childhood home, that is. The mornings there were always filled with the cooing of mating doves. Ma and I would sit by the windows in the front room, mostly in silence for Ma and I never had much to say to each other, and listen to them as we did our little bits of work. Mostly, I did embroidery—delicate shadow work on gauzy organza or the regimented cross-stitch on matty cloth—while Ma knitted, her needles flashing in the morning sun. Thick, delicious sweaters she turned out in days, in readiness for the cold winters. I will ask her to knit you a bundle, don't worry, you will never be cold.

I sit in your room, in which I had never sat before, immersed in your presence, and although it is still empty, only the computer table and chair in the corner, I feel so full, so rich and laden with hope. Since July, I have been carrying around with me an unremitting ache of loneliness—sunrises and other things can only do so much to assuage that—and it is here, only here, that I feel I am not alone.

Yet another place I have discovered after your father's sudden departure is my bed. *Our* bed, I had always thought of it as, the one my father had made from solid teak for my wedding, just a little bit dated now with the fashion veering towards dark veneers—wenge and ebony and all those foreign woods. Your father loved it, more than I did actually, which surprised me for he was always so careful to be in vogue; for my part I found it too high and too wide, I would have liked it narrower so that your father and I could be closer but every time I spoke of selling it and getting a new one he would lose his temper so we have had it with us all these years.

Now, of course, he has abandoned his bed for a new one, without a thought. Does he ever miss the bed, I wonder. That he does not miss me yet goes without saying although he still calls every week to ask if I was all right for money and if I needed anything. He is careful about the superficial things, he always has been a great one for form and anyway, our families in Assam still do not know and this, after all, is an arranged marriage. When he calls his voice is friendly, now that he has escaped he can afford to relax, but I can hear that he does not miss me. I have not told him about you so he does not miss you yet. I want to tell him properly, in our house, when things are cleared up finally.

Anyway, my bedroom which looks out on to the veranda that runs along the front of the flat, is a place I had never spent much time in before. Barring the nights, of course, but that was different and it was quite another world we were immersed in then.

In the daytime now, I find it is a tranquil place, with the bed made up neatly and the sunlight filtering through the shrubs on the veranda, plants I have grown with so much love and determination. I have taken to having my evening cup of coffee—decaffeinated, don't worry—there, in the cane chair near the windows. The sun loses most of its harshness by then and the gentler rays light up the plants delicately. Sometimes, if I am lucky, a pair of purple-rumped sunbirds alights on the fountain grass in the pot in the corner to peck at the ears of red-purple seeds. The first time I saw them I almost jumped out of my chair to go call your father at work to tell him about them—after all, he was crazier about birds than I was—but then I remembered and I have to tell you, I sat down on my bed and wept like a baby.

These days I have also taken to doing something I am not accustomed to. I now take an afternoon nap, lying down on my bed, the outside world shielded from me momentarily by gauzy sheer curtains. The first time I did that, I felt odd. It should have been familiar to me, coming from Assam where the afternoon siesta was an inviolable part of daily life, but although I had participated in it, taking care not to make any noise during those two hours when the household lay inert, submerged in slumber, I never gave in to sleep myself, preferring instead to read a novel or study. Now, I find as soon as I lie down, my eyes close and I sink into an exhausted sleep. It must be all those hormones racing up and down my veins these days. I wake up feeling groggy, disoriented, as if I am emerging from a fantastic world far away from my life here. In fact, that was why when I felt that first flutter in my pelvis last week, I thought I was imagining it until you kicked again and I knew for certain that you were there, calling out for me.

My first thought, as I sat up, was to call and tell your father; after all I still loved him, it was he who had said that he had stopped loving me and besides I knew how much he would love you. I almost called, the cell phone was in my hand, but I didn't. Two things happened: I felt a black anger surge through me and although I tried to calm down—my anger would not do you any good—it still was a while before my hands stopped shaking. I was startled by this hot rush—I do not tend towards anger usually, but maybe it was the hormones again. In the aftermath of the anger, a new thought struck me. I was certain that as soon as I told your father about you, he would come home, back to me. And I did not want him to do that. I wanted him back, more urgently than I admitted even to myself, yet, at the same time, I wanted him to come back to me, *for me.* Not to you. Make no mistake, I am not competing with you for his love—there is no competition here at all. He will adore you, you will be the centre of his world, but I want to be assured of his old love for me before he comes back, that same love I have grown accustomed to these seven years.

I put the phone carefully back on the bedside table and lay down again. Another deception. But then I have been dealing in so many deceptions since I met your father and in these last four months I have had a great deal of practice in that fine art. I have told Mary, who cooks and cleans for me, and Vincent, the driver, that your father was away abroad on a project, something he has to do quite often, so they haven't questioned it. When his parents or mine call, I tell them the same thing. My mother, who has a sharp eye, murmurs that this is an unusually long trip, I agree and say, Yes, this is a highly unusual situation.

The hardest lie to pull off was the meeting with our doctor. When the pregnancy kit repeatedly showed up positive, three and a half months ago, I had no choice but to go see Dr Joseph. She was delighted to be able to confirm my pregnancy—after all, she had been with us through every step of our struggle to conceive you—and was surprised to find your father missing. A trip abroad, I said, smiling, but when I arrived for every subsequent meeting alone she displayed some consternation. I refused to take her cue, telling her instead how jubilant your father was and that he couldn't be happier.

Curiously, I don't find it hard to conceal my pregnant state from my parents, not even my mother; I have never shared anything of consequence in my life with them anyway. As for friends and neighbours, fortunately, I am not showing at all; I am still thin and my stomach flat as always. So, even if I were to meet my friends they would not know.

I have not met any of our friends, not that I have too many, for the last four months. We have spoken on the telephone; that is not so difficult, it is easy to hide behind a phone but will I be able to look them in the eye? I know of one friend who would have undoubtedly found me out, but she is gone now, Joya is dead and gone; she has left me permanently, there is no hope of getting her back at all.

The phone rings early this morning as I sit on the veranda, sipping my cup of green tea. I am intent upon a pair of doves that sit on the electric line across the street, billing and cooing at each other. The ringing of the phone fractures my scrutiny and I am upset; this feeling deepens as the name flashes on the phone screen. Sonia. I glance at my watch quickly; it is only half past seven, I am tempted to let the phone ring on, it is early enough for me to claim being asleep. But Sonia will ring every hour on the hour until I answer. I take the call.

'Hello,' Sonia says, 'hope I did not wake you?'

'No, not at all,' I say, 'I was just having tea.'

'Ron is still away?'

'Yes,' I say, truthfully.

Sonia is enthusiastic. 'Great,' she replies. 'Then we can meet for lunch. Are you free today?'

It was no use. How long could I hide?

'Yes, I am,' I answer. 'Where shall we meet?'

As soon as I say that I know I will regret it. Without breaking stride Sonia suggests a rooftop café near her house; she sweetens the offer by telling me we can spend some time browsing in the bookshop that is below and I murmur agreement while inside me resentment begins to flare up again.

No, I won't allow it; it is my own fault—there are so many restaurants this side of town, I should have suggested one of them.

A flock of parrots have settled in the clump of peacock flower trees in the park across the street; they are a raucous lot and their screeching and frisky play makes me smile.

This park—I used to call it 'our park' and I would like to still call it that—was the one thing your father and I completely agreed upon. I remember, six years ago, when we began scouting for houses to buy, how we had quarrelled: we argued and shouted, I wept while your father thundered; I banged doors and he threw dishes. We had all these disparate requirements, you see: your father wanted a flat in the centre of town, I had no such need but my stipulation was that it should be in a quiet street and really, there was no such place in the area your father wanted to be in; he wanted certain things in a building—marble floors, wooden door and window frames as opposed to the metal ones seen more and more these days—which to me were irrelevant. I wanted a nice home too, mind you, but my wants and his were like parallel lines and I despaired of ever finding a flat.

Then one day, Shabbir, the broker, called to say he had found a flat in an older building, in the right side of Richmond Town; he said it had many things we were looking for, so would we be interested.

Your father was driving, I was in the passenger seat and the broker in the back, from where he was telling your father where to go. We turned left off the main arterial road that sliced through the neighbourhood and then a few buildings away turned right into a smaller lane. The usual afternoon din—blaring horns, tyres squealing, snatches of music— seemed to have skirted this area and it was almost unsettling for we had grown accustomed to there being a symphony of

jahnavi barua

noise in the background. To my left I could see a green area but it was unclear as to what it really was: a large private garden, a private park or a public one. As your father parked the car I looked around the place—the road led on past us and turned left. Again, it was so empty I was surprised.

'Dead-end road, madam,' Shabbir volunteered.

That explained the strange hush. I was beginning to get excited now and turned to look up at the building. It was not new, it would have been around six, maybe seven years old but it had been looked after well and had an air of confidence. You may ask what exactly I mean by that, and I may not be able to tell you precisely what I saw, but let's say it was like a lady with good bones; she looked good and would age well in the years to come. There was—thank goodness—marble on the floor and the window and door frames were made of teak, polished to a soft gloss.

The particular flat we had come to see was on the top floor. When Shabbir opened the door, we found ourselves in a small lobby-like area, six feet square, and as we stood there uncertainly and looked across the empty expanse of the drawing room I had a compelling feeling that we had come home, that this was the place your father and I were looking for.

On the far side were a set of French windows through which the green area we had seen briefly from the car was visible. The slanting rays of the evening sun reached in through the bare windows and seemed to draw us to them. As we stood by the windows Shabbir fumbled with the lock and as he did I looked out and saw what you and I are looking at now: the park—I knew then that it was a park, there was a sandpit with swings and ladders, and a fountain in the centre and all round the periphery wound a walking track, half hidden in places by the lush green growth. Your father was standing beside me and I don't know what came over me, for we have never been expressive in public, but I gripped his hand as if to urge him to decide on this flat that I had seen so little of yet. Your father shook my hand off and turned away, into the dim inside of the apartment. He must have been satisfied with what he encountered for he came out beaming and I smiled back at him.

'A little bit of paint and polish and it should look great,' your father said and suddenly all of us were laughing. We leaned our elbows on the metal railing and gazed out at the park, all three of us—your father, Shabbir and I—and were silent for a while. That was how we found our home. The park was what had decided your father; he ran in it every morning, dressed to the hilt in his red Nike shorts and hooded sweat shirt and his four-thousand-rupee Nike Air running shoes. Every evening, after work, he would retreat to the deep veranda in front of the drawing room and lie there, in his cane lounger, a cold glass of rum in his hands. I joined him sometimes but mostly I was uncomfortable there. Every building on our little right-angled street had balconies overlooking the park; they all looked into each other and we were as visible as the man on the road.

'How funny you are!' your father always said in exasperation but there I was, strange, I suppose, but having grown up in a house that was expertly screened from neighbours on both sides by impenetrable tangles of bamboo and hibiscus and kothona and chompa, I was uneasy about being looked at by strangers. Noises were another matter; noises that cut their way through these green barriers could safely be ignored. There was no concrete evidence linking them to you, one could even pretend they were from the television, and it was easy enough in the morning light to look one's neighbour in the eye and smile. But to be stared at was more than I could bear.

Inside the park however, I was anonymous, one of a large flock of women bedecked in colourful track pants and fitted tee-shirts. Every evening at five I would arrive there for my fifteen rounds in forty minutes. After that I rewarded myself with a tranquil fifteen minutes by the fountain. It was there that I had first met Preetha, and what a fateful meeting that was and what a wonderful person she is, you will love her, but more about that later. I have much to do before setting out for lunch with Sonia.

A key turns in a lock and my skin tingles. But it is only my Mary, who has a spare key so she can let herself in even when I am not at home.

'Good morning, madam,' Mary's broad smile lights up the room.

Her enthusiasm lifts my mood. 'Good morning,' I smile back.

Mary is a small, neat person—much shorter than me for I stand at five feet six inches—with an arrestingly beautiful face: classically oval with high cheek bones, her bones are lovely and over them is stretched delicious skin, dark and luminous. Her bindi—bottu as it is called here—glows on her high forehead. Mary is not young, she is over fifty, but her spirit is robust and she manages to somehow rouse me out of my black moods. Seven years we have known each other now and have grown accustomed to each other. In a way, we have transcended the traditional mistress–servant relationship. She has been steadfast through these years, none of your appraising-the-neighbours-for-better-pay here, I do not worry about her disappearing from my house and reappearing in a neighbour's house next morning. She is loyal, a rare attribute these days. You will like her, she will sing you to sleep, one of those lilting Tamil melodies she hums around the house.

'Breakfast, madam?' Mary says as she clears away the empty cup of tea.

'Yes, please, Mary.' I would have refused before but I have you to think of now. So it is oatmeal porridge in the mornings for me these days, sprinkled with raisins, high in iron they are, and nuts filled with the good omega-3 fatty acids and a glass of fresh juice, power-packed with vitamins. The thought of these lovely nutrients swirling along in my blood finding their way to you makes me so happy.

There are many things you have to do for others no matter how averse you are to them, you will understand this in time. This morning I am setting out to do one of them—meeting Sonia. She is the wife of your father's boss—senior colleague, they call them these days but that does not change the fact that they are bosses—and friend, Rahul Kapoor. In the beginning, my reluctance to socialize, as he called it, with your father's friends had been a recurrent point of conflict between the two of us. We spoke different languages, his friends and I; maybe it was because of the small town I came from, but many of them came from small towns too. Maybe, I thought after one weary evening, I just spoke a language that was strange to most people. One day your father sat me down. He was not angry that day, he was just tired, I think, for he simply said, 'You had better get used to this.'

Odd, but that evening he sounded uncannily like my mother and that was what switched something on in my brain and I saw with amazing clarity that this was my life and I would have to acclimatize. For better or worse, excuse the cliché.

From that day on I made a robust effort to mingle, to blend into the brilliantly coloured throngs of women and men that floated in and out of your father's social circle. I found I managed; I did not have too much to say to them, but I could dig up the odd piece of conversation and to both your father's astonishment and mine, I began to be considered interesting, funny even, for I thought so differently from them all.

'Mary, will you dust for me today?' I feel a twinge of guilt as I ask; your father was fastidious about the dusting and liked me to do it. But I was setting out, after all, to do something else he insisted on—meeting Sonia regularly.

A traffic jam does odd things to people. Your father would begin to sweat, even with the air conditioner turned up to maximum; he would turn pink in the face and then begin to swear. I do hope you don't have to hear him swearing, ever. But then, he was always in a hurry; he always had so much to do. Then there are others, many women among them, who begin to fidget—they twist their rings round and round on their fingers or pick at their mobile phones, checking messages, missed calls—as soon as the traffic even begins to slow down. Sometimes I think I must be the aberration for I am utterly relaxed in a car—not if I have to drive, I have a horror of driving although I can—and a traffic pile-up never even begins to upset me. That was because I had nowhere to get to and mostly nothing to do, your father would always point out, and he was right, I have to agree. A good thing considering the chaos the traffic in Bangalore is mired in these days.

Someone—one of these lifestyle gurus—had said that a traffic jam presented a person with a number of opportunities and it was up to each one of us what we did with them. If one delved hard enough, this frustrating impediment could be turned to one's advantage; this was time that could be used to think, to meditate, to analyse or just relax. I couldn't agree more; this is one philosophy I had evolved for myself, long ago, when still a girl: there was little use in fighting against something that was unassailable. It was best that one worked around it.

The restaurant, café really, is ten kilometres across some of the busiest roads in town. Traffic moves at the pace of ants drunk on fruit punch, and although I am not riled by the slowness of it, I find I am edgy this morning. I smooth the black knit kameez I am wearing repeatedly although it is non-wrinkle. Should I have worn my usual jeans instead? The risk I ran then was that you might show, Sonia has sharp eyes. She has eyes that see everything and she has no inhibitions about saying unpleasant things, couched, mind you, in the blandest of words and most deceptive of tones. You have to watch out for her. I am always in battle mode when I am to see her; today I have put on my mask carefully: a refreshing layer of moisturizer and then an instant perfector cream that evens out the skin—your father always said I didn't need it, I was lucky to have the clear skin of the women of my part of the country, but it fortifies me—and I have painted my eyelids with eyeshadow and darkened my eyes with kajal. There is strawberry-flavoured gloss on my lips that I lick now and then, you would like the taste, I think.

There is no doubt in my mind that Sonia knows about your father's misadventures; Rahul and your father are good friends and besides they work in the same office. I can hardly take the trip-abroad line with her. But, you see, that is the great thing about Sonia: she possesses the ability to blank out something she is not willing to talk about. Like the time she had proposed we all go to Goa together during the Puja break—this was the year we had met, five years ago—for a holiday. I worked myself into a lather of excitement, I had never been to Goa and so looked forward to being there with your father. All your father said was, 'Don't believe everything you hear', and I dismissed him as jaded and cynical but Puja came and went and Sonia came back from Goa tanned and sleek and happy as a seal in water and she did not ever mention that she had invited us along and I learnt to hold my tongue and my thoughts in check.

Expectations. This is an unfashionable word in the world I live in here. It is a point of pride, a badge, women especially, like to flaunt, this *lack* of expectations. If you expect the slightest thing from anyone you are made to feel as if you are a parasite, a person so demanding it is impossible to have a relationship with you. So I learnt to throw most of my expectations out of the window. I am warning you though, I have a lot of expectations of you, I don't care if you let me down and break my heart but only with these expectations, darling, can I love you.

The interior of the bookshop is cold and still; I have goosebumps on my forearms. There. I can see Sonia at the back of the shop; she has a book in her hand and is bending down to look at something, her sleek head with its short, cropped hair bent delicately on her long neck. She straightens up and turns around in the same motion and we are now eye to eye and her mouth rearranges itself into a smile and she begins to move towards me. I begin to walk forward too, but at the same time feel ridiculously awkward and reluctant as if impelled towards her by some force outside myself.

'Darling!' Sonia bends down to kiss me, twice, once on each cheek. I raise my face obediently and do the same.

She then steps back, holding me by both elbows—the book is tucked under her arm now—and sighs. 'You look fabulous, as always. How do you do it?'

'Hard work.' I laugh. Sonia is waiting for the compliment to be returned but I am in a perverse mood today.

'What are you buying?' I ask.

Sonia is dismissive. 'Only a cookbook.' She turns towards the non-fiction section. 'I'll see you in a bit then,' she says.

I begin with the As and work my way down the bookshelves. I stop at C; I have not read *Disgrace* yet and would have liked to have browsed through it but somehow today my heart is not in it. Still, I wander down the aisle looking at the familiar names; I am compelled to stop at K, Kawabata. I caress the spine of the book as if stroking the hand of an old and beloved friend. I cannot forget the girl in his book, *The Sound of the Mountain*. Her relationship with her father-in-law haunts me; is it possible that there can be only friendship between a man and woman unrelated by blood? I had been so deeply unsettled by the book when I first read it; your father had only laughed. He said I had lived so little in the real world that the fictional appeared so very significant to me.

No, I will not buy a book today. I will try and live in my life instead.

'Are you done?' Sonia calls over a bookshelf. 'Shall we head upstairs?'

'Sure.' I wait by the lift as Sonia pays for her book.

The café is on the third floor, above the tree line, and there is a glorious view of the canopy spread patchily over apartment buildings and houses. Without thought I head towards the open area of the rooftop.

'It's too hot in the sun, Kaberi,' Sonia says and she sits down heavily at a table in the enclosed section.

I turn around and sit down across her. Below us, in the street, cars move back and forth relentlessly but here it is calm, we are, for the moment, safe, cloistered in this glass enclosure encircled by green trees and blue sky. Few of the trees are in flower; it is too early for the pink tabebuias, they would begin blossoming in a month or so, by late November, and it was much too late or much too early, depending how you looked at it, for the yellow ones and the gulmohars that flamed across the city in early summer. Deeper down though, through gaps in the tree cover I catch sight of crimson ixoras, the dome-like flower clusters staining the green bushes.

Sonia lights a cigarette. Of their own accord my hands move to protect my stomach. I cough.

'Oh, sorry,' Sonia reaches forward and stubs out her cigarette in a quick, brutal movement on a saucer. 'I keep forgetting you are allergic.'

'No, no, I am sorry!' I laugh as I worry about you squirming inside me. I shift in my seat and with my right hand push my hair behind my ear. It is too long; I can feel it tickling the nape of my neck, I will have to get it cut.

'Nice cut,' Sonia says as if she can read my thoughts, 'this layered blunt really suits you. And it is so much in fashion.'

'Ron likes it this way,' I say and then I am suddenly awkward. Sonia does not even blink.

'So, what are you up to these days? We hardly see you, what do you do with Ron away?'

What I always did. 'The usual,' I say, 'the house, the plants, you know.'

'Hats off to you, ya,' Sonia laughs, 'you are so happy pottering about in your own home.'

The waiter is now beside us; I order vegetarian pasta, an aglio e olio, while Sonia chooses the mixed seafood pasta. That is my favourite dish but now with you I cannot risk eating shellfish.

Sonia fills me in on her doings: the dinners, the lunches,

the art openings she has been to in the last few months. It is a hectic life and it suits her. I listen to her carefully trying to catch in every inflection of her every word, in the cadence of her conversation, a hint that she knew about your father and my recent estrangement. Nothing. It is as if she is oblivious to the situation.

After a point, as I always end up doing, I find myself floating away from our table; I am present enough to comment on her doings, I offer a few comments of my own but I am looking at the cloudless sky and the still green leaves of the trees. I think of you and feel an unstoppable flood of longing. I want to hold you tight in my arms.

Sonia and I share a tiramisu and then as we split the bill she says we must do this more often, I should stay in touch. I tell her I will and I mean it. When your father comes back he will see that I have kept our lives intact, the way he liked me to.

Sonia's belt buckle digs into my stomach as she gives me a hug on the steps outside the shop, I step back abruptly, afraid for you.

Before heading home I stop at the nursery near the café; my stock of organic manure for the plants is dipping low. Along with the manure, I buy a kilogram of something called *Trichoderma Viridae*—it is a live fungus that works antagonistically against harmful fungus in soil. A soil conditioner it is called; I smile, it reminds me of hair conditioner. Another stop at a supermarket I like on CMH Road; there I pick up dried apricots—yellow foods are especially good for your dividing cells—and prunes and frozen fish. With your father gone it is too much trouble to buy fresh fish from Johnson Market.

The next doctor's appointment is tomorrow, I want to be strong for it.

Mary is gone when I get back. The flat is closed, it is hushed and still inside and inexplicably, my eyes fill. I close the door behind me and even before I can put my bag down I am crying. What did I expect? I know Mary leaves by lunchtime, she always does, but somehow I thought she would be here today.

I put the shopping away. I change out of the churidar kameez into a kaftan, still weeping. Mary has drawn the curtains against the afternoon sun. My bedroom is filled with a dim, underwater light, the sun filtering through the moss-green curtains; it is as if I am submerged in a noiseless watery world. I feel you kick, are you tired? I must lie down then, now.

This silence, this particular kind of silence, where the very air seems to be frozen, makes me afraid. I have been afraid of it ever since Joya. It has been three years but even now this hush makes the hair stand up on my forearms. That had been my first glimpse of death, you see; of course, I had seen dead bodies before, Joya herself had taken me to the Anatomy dissection hall in the medical college where they cut up cadavers to study them, but that had been different. I hadn't known what death meant until that moment, three years ago, when I walked into Joya's house. What struck me, what marked that morning indelibly in my heart was the silence that had descended over that house and muffled its very heartbeat. No one cried—Joya's mother, Bina Mahi, had not cried, and that had arrested the tears of all the others around her, but what a look of anguish there had been on her face, as if her entire world had been torn asunder and nothing could ever piece it together again. The blood ran cold in my veins that sunny morning; it was so still, there was no movement in that room, not even a curtain shifted in the wind, and I felt fear choking my throat. There was no body, you know, the blast had shred everything in that bus to pieces. I could not even look upon Joya's face for that last time.

Would you like to hear about Joya? But I must be crazy to start with the end, let me begin at the other end, at the beginning, so you will understand.

Joya was my friend. No, that is not adequate at all; she was so much more. I would like to say she was my sister but then we were created of different flesh so let me call her my alter ego, for it was difficult sometimes to distinguish where Joya ended and I began, where we flowed into one another, a pair of underground streams.

Our houses stood next to each other in one of the older localities in the heart of Guwahati town; our grandfathers had built these houses and our fathers had grown up in them, good friends, almost brothers, and then we were born, two months apart, and fell into line—we grew up together, close friends, and assumed arrogantly that we would remain so and that our children after us would be friends too.

Joya and I were together almost every waking moment, even when we were infants, two, three months old. Either Bina Mahi would send Joya across to our house with Joymati, her maid, or else I would be taken to Joya's house by Golapi Bai, my maid. We were good together, even then, Joya and I. Although younger, she was the more adventurous one and led the two of us in play; she would crawl under the kothali chompa bush in the corner of her front garden and there, squeezed together under the green branches redolent with the intensely sweet scent of the chompa blossoms, we would pretend we were in a green cave and play house until dragged out by some frantic adult. Snakes frequented that area, I learnt later, enticed there by the sweet-smelling flowers, but even that knowledge did not deter Joya who would wander down there again and again, with me in tow. I learnt to be brave from her, how not to cry when I fell and scraped my knee, while she learnt from me to be watchful and patient. We were the perfect foils for each other.

Those early years seem incredible now, they were so perfect. We grew up without fuss, the two of us—took our first steps one after the other in succession, then spoke our first words, Joya first and then I—and no one bothered to document or even remember when it was that we did, unlike today when every move a baby makes is recorded in a book, a compact disc or on film. That reminds me, I saw an absolutely delicious baby book in the bookshop today, yellow cover the colour of sunshine; I must get it for you. Anyway, we grew up and then it was time for school.

The local convent school was about a kilometre away from us and it was there that we were both admitted the year we turned three. From the quiet lane that our homes stood on we had to turn on to the busy main road that led past the long pond and then turn into a quieter road where the school building stood, silent and threatening, behind high iron gates. The first two years our mothers ferried us back and forth to school in rickshaws but the year we turned five we were made to walk there. I will tell you all about what went on in that school and how we fared there those twelve years but let me tell you now about the walk to school. Until we were in class four—we were nine that year—Joymati and Golapi Bai accompanied us to school. Then, one day my father said, 'Now the girls are old enough. They can walk alone to school, I will speak to Bipul.' I had been sitting at the dining table doing my homework by candlelight, I remember, there was a power cut hence the candle, and Ma was sitting to my left, supervising me. I heard her draw her breath in sharply and exhale just as quickly and the flame flared up in alarm.

My heart fluttered in my breast like a nervous bird but my face showed nothing. Yes, I had learnt the art of masquerade even before I had met your father; it would be unfair of me to blame my skills on him. What was it, you may ask, that

jahnavi barua

aroused this fear? It was a teashop. An ordinary teashop—three walls of bamboo, the front mostly open, closed at night by a hinged bamboo flap, and a roof of corrugated tin. It stood at the corner where our lane led onto the main road; it was impossible to avoid for that was the only way out of our dead-end road.

From early morning—in our part of the world the day began early—till nightfall, packs of young men, boys, hung around the shop. They lounged around on the battered wooden benches inside the shop's dim interior and frequently spilled over onto the dusty road. From there they amused themselves by picking on passing women. I say women, but really they harassed any female between the age of six and sixty. Joya and I were easy, favoured targets for we consistently passed them morning and afternoon. The presence of Joymati and Golapi Bai had reined them in only a little; despite Joymati's sharp tongue they still called out lewd, uncouth words that cut my skin like so many razor blades.

Joya made that walk possible for me: she walked on the outside, back straight and chin raised and whenever a shout or cry came our way she lifted her chin higher and pretended not to hear. My hands shook and my knees wobbled but the fact of Joya walking by my side, deflecting the venom being thrown at us, tamped down my fear.

Courage can be learnt, I realized. Joya taught me well and I have, I think, been a good student.

Dr Joseph is pleased with me. She smiles at me from across the table; behind her, through the large glass window, I can see the spreading arms of a rain tree, luminous in the afternoon sun. This is why I always come to see her at the clinic and not at the hospital; here it is almost as if I am visiting a good friend and the changes taking place inside me are only incidental, peripheral to our actual purpose of meeting. There are no unsavoury smells, not even in the glossy, green, apple-scented restroom where I collect my mandatory sample of urine in a plastic cup. The nurse at the blood collection table, dressed in a snowy white lab coat, could easily be mistaken for an attendant at a luxury cosmetic store. Although, I must explain myself here, again it is not the laminations of luxury that draw me here, but the illusion that I am here for something other than this condition I am in. Even the jab I am given now, the tetanus toxoid, does not take away from this at all.

'Eighteen weeks now, Kaberi,' Dr Joseph sits upright in her chair, elbows on the table, fingers joined together above in a steeple.

'Yes,' I smile.

'You are doing well, sweetie.' Rising up from her chair in a fluid movement, Dr Joseph beckons me to the weighing scales behind her desk.

I stand on them obediently.

'Fifty-seven kilos. Very nice.' Dr Joseph ushers me to the examination bed and as I climb on and lie down I do a swift mental calculation. I had been fifty-five kilos the day I first came to her so I had put on two kilos so far. Almost textbook perfect.

I untie the drawstring of my salwar. Dr Joseph pushes it down gently and with light, gentle movements of the side of her left hand she measures up from my pubis. She stops at a point midway between the bony prominence and my navel.

'There,' she says and taking my hand, places it there, 'this is how big Baby is now.'

She means my womb, of course; I have been reading diligently since you appeared on the scene and I know that in the eighteenth week you are only about six inches long; the rest of the bump is my fattened womb, pulsing with blood and muscle, guarding you until the day it will force you out of its tenacious embrace.

This afternoon there is no internal examination. My blood pressure is checked, breasts given a once-over and I am off the table.

I settle myself in the comfortable chair again. Dr Joseph is filling in my history sheet. I watch in admiration as her slim fingers with their meticulously short nails move confidently across the sheet covering it with large, loopy cursive writing. They say the worse the writing, the better the doctor, but I disagree: Dr Joseph is a brilliant doctor and so was Joya. Joya with her assertive, square, clear print.

The doctor's voice breaks into my thoughts.

'Let's do something today,' she says, 'let's do an ultrasound.'

The surprise must have shown on my face.

'Do you want to wait for Ranjit?'

'No,' I say, 'but the bladder?'

'Why don't you do something?' Dr Joseph says, as she comes around her desk to steer me out of the room. 'Why don't you drink some water here and then head out somewhere nearby for some shopping? Come back in a couple of hours.'

I take the good doctor's advice and I ask Vincent to take me to the nearest mall. It is one designed only for women; the only one in the city and quite possibly the only one in the country. That is not why I am here though; it is the most convenient so I have come. But I have no intention of browsing, my feet ache and there is a heaviness in my limbs, something I am feeling increasingly these days. I plan to sit in the central atrium where there are benches placed in a rough circle and read my book; I always carry one in my oversized handbag. There are only a few women in the open space as I sit down;

it is mid-afternoon on a weekday after all. The crowds come in on the weekends.

It is unexpectedly peaceful here. I look around the gleaming shopfronts, Nike Woman, Adidas for Women, Benetton and even a store for the large woman; something about their cheerful expectancy—they are waiting for something good to happen, a customer to walk in, a big sale to be accomplished—is buoyant. I feel cheerful but do I feel safe? As safe as anywhere else, I reckon. Large crowds of women have never made me feel particularly safe and now I know I was right to feel that way.

The book I am reading is a sad one, at least it is so far. I hesitated before starting it for I did not want you to feel any uncalled-for grief trickling through my veins. But I began it anyway, and once I did, I could not stop. It is about a couple who have lost a child. There was no dramatic kidnapping or snowstorm or trek in a jungle. The child was lost in a supermarket, on a very ordinary shopping outing on a very ordinary day. That is precisely what is so terrifying, the possibility of unimagined dangers in a familiar setting. Joya always laughed at how I had absolutely no fear of ghosts and other such manifestations yet I was terrified of burglars and rapists and other more mundane terrors. After the child is lost the parents fall out badly; it is natural, I suppose, the mother blamed the father who had been in charge of the child but I itched for her to back down, to yield and see and acknowledge the agony the father was going through. They could be sad together, they could hold each other up.

Your father and I had no such reason to develop a rift. I never gave him a reason. And yet. Maybe I should have been a different person; maybe I should have been more assertive, more argumentative, less willing to acquiesce, but that has never been my way. Even when Joya would work herself into a lather over my submissiveness I never gave in—I did not see conflict as obligatory in every situation. Things could be worked around. Or could they? I don't know these days, I am not sure of my convictions any more. All I know is that things are never what they seem to be, that nothing is permanent in the way I knew it.

My bladder is calling out to me urgently now; you have been very silent this past hour but they do say a full bladder impedes contraction of the womb. I need to leave right now. It is time to head back to the clinic.

The technician pulls my salwar down as I stare up at the ceiling. My breath comes in fast, shallow spurts; this is something I have been preparing myself for—my first sighting of you—and yet now when I am on the brink, I am afraid. Terrified of what I will see, and underneath that terror, underscoring it until it screams out to me, is an intense guilt. Your father should be standing here right now; this is a moment I am stealing from him that I can never give back. He makes me do these things, he makes me, I tell you. I would love to have him here beside me but he has to come back—he should have come back.

Dr Joseph strides into the room. She sits down beside me and squeezes a little jelly from a tube on to my stomach. I flinch.

Instantly she is solicitous. 'Are you okay, darling?'

'Yes, only it is cold.'

The probe is on my stomach now, digging in a little. Images appear on the monitor in front of us. Patches of light and dark and cloudy greys that don't make sense to me.

'There.' Dr Joseph sounds satisfied. 'Can you see the spine there?'

I strain to see and when she runs a finger in a curve over a line of lightness and denseness I begin to see. Yes, I can see you now. There is your backbone, little knobbly bones joined together curled tight like a little shrimp. My throat contracts. My gaze is drawn to a familiar structure—could it be that?

'And that is a foot,' Dr Joseph confirms it.

A big foot, I begin to smile, just like your father's.

The park is deserted when I get back home. The sun has set and the shadows are gathering thick and fast under the trees and low bushes. I have missed my evening walk today.

Before I go to bed I take out the ultrasound film and hold it against the bedside lamp. There you are, my darling, your back fitted perfectly against one wall of my womb, your big foot pressed against another. Are you sucking your thumb? They say you can do that now, they say you can hear me.

The curtain flutters in a sudden breeze. I feel a touch on my shoulder.

I must be crazy but I don't feel alone tonight; there are ghosts looking over my shoulder—Joya, without doubt, and someone else. Is it your father?

For the first time in weeks I feel that I will sleep well. I will dream of Joya and Kaziranga, good dreams. I will wake up plump with happiness and tell you about them tomorrow.

D reams can be dreamt in colour and you can smell things in them too.

When I wake up the room is suffused with the peculiar spicy-sweet smell of the kothali chompa—I close my eyes and the waxy green of the flowers pushes against my lids. I am lying on my side and I stretch a little and then curl back into a tight half-circle. I am—no, we are, you and I—moths in the warm cocoon of the duvet; soon we will spread our wings and fly away.

You father does not believe in dreams; he never sees any he always says but I have my own theory about that. I am sure he has dreams, everybody does, but your father wipes them clean out of his mind. Weak-minded, he thinks dreamers are, too willing to submit to fanciful ideas and for once Joya and he have the same opinion. Joya saw dreams, she admitted to that, but she never remembered them. All she could say when she finally broke free of them was if they were sad dreams or happy. And either way it made no difference to her, she would plunge into her day in utter disregard of them. I can never do that: to begin with, I remember every vivid detail; the arrangement of rooms I move through in my unconscious state, the quality of sunlight outside, the briskness of the wind;

the expressions on people's faces as they look at me can sometimes make me cry when I wake up. So many mornings I awake to find the pillowslip wet with salty tears. My days and nights, dreams and real life, are woven together in a delicate pattern; without fail the first few moments of waking up set the tone for the day that follows.

This morning I am overcome by an inexplicable lassitude; it is not unpleasant, in a peculiar way it is comforting, the sharp edges of things are blurred and I am disoriented, just mildly so, as if I have drunk a glass of wine too fast. The fragrance of the chompa keeps coming back to me.

I turn over, onto my back. There is a flutter in my pelvis, as if in response to this shift. You are awake. Do you sleep at all, I wonder, or are you perpetually in the stuporous state I am in now? They say you can hear me now, and I will sing to you, my sweet. But now I have to hurry to the bathroom, all your wriggling is doing me no good.

Mary cooks me a big breakfast. She carries it out on a tray to the veranda, where I am sitting. A big plate of sausages, fried egg, buttered toast and a tall glass of juice. And banana. I do hate banana but I will eat it for you.

'My goodness, Mary,' I smile up at her, 'you will make me very fat.'

Mary beams in response. 'No, madam,' she says, 'you need it.'

A chill runs up my spine at her words. Does Mary know about you? I must be over-sensitive; Mary always maintained I needed fattening, it is nothing new.

I am still contemplating the food laid out before me when the doorbell rings. Mary opens the door; I cannot see it from where I am sitting unless I lean forward but I can hear her voice. She is laughing and when she speaks her voice is pitched higher than usual; she is happy to see someone.

The cane chair creaks in protest as I ease my weight forward; I still cannot see but I do not have to now, the blood rushes to my face at the familiar timbre. I fall back quickly in the chair, I want to disappear; the thought of him seeing me like this—dishevelled, unprepared—makes me cringe. My hand shakes as I smooth my damp palm over my tousled hair. I cinch the belt of my block-printed housecoat tighter around my waist.

'Hi.'

I squint up at him, your father. 'Hello,' I say, 'this is unexpected. You could have called first.'

'What for?' Your father seems surprised. 'Since when have you developed an appetite?' He sits down across me.

Before I can answer he picks up a fork and expertly spears a brown sausage. He delivers it neatly to his mouth and then reaches for another.

Just as his fork swoops down I snatch the plate up; I am trembling with the effort and the breath is tangled inside my chest.

'What the hell?' Ron freezes, his arms are outstretched, elbows bent, the palms of his hands facing up. The fork in his right hand catches the sunlight and glints fiercely. For a moment I think I will be sick and then it passes.

'Mary will get you some food if you want,' my voice sounds odd, even to me. I speak in a rush, the words flooding into each other, the tone flat.

Your father laughs. It is not a kind sound. 'Oh my God,' he says, 'we are touchy today, aren't we?'

There is no answer to that and I do not bother making one. Very carefully, I set the plate down on the coffee table between us; my wrists ache with the effort.

Mary has put the morning papers out next to the food. I look at them sideways; I focus on the headlines, that should do it.

Even in this effort I am to be thwarted—a small caption on the right side catches my eye: red alert in Assam as the countdown begins to the raising day of one of the insurgent groups.

'Look at me, Kaberi,' your father's voice is calm now.

So, I obey him; I raise my eyes and look at him for the first time in four months. He looks good, your father, he looks even better than before, she is looking after him well; he is dressed in a suit although it is not cold enough for it but your father was always the stylish one. You cannot see him yet, little one, but soon, very soon.

'There is something we have to discuss,' your father says. He does not hold my gaze.

I do not say anything.

Your father leans forward; his hands are clasped together and I see his knuckles are white. 'I want a divorce.'

For the first time, or at least as far as I can remember, my dreams have let me down; I had dreamt of Joya and Kaziranga and yet. Yet, I did wake up with the scent of the chompa in the air. That alluring scent that enticed hidden dangers.

I am afraid to look at him, so I turn my head towards the park. A solitary pink tabebuia is in bloom on the corner near the main road; I am incredulous, I hadn't seen it yesterday. Could it have burst into bloom overnight or has my attention been slipping? Good thing I was seeing things in soft focus today; the word your father had hurled so unexpectedly at me did not hurt so much.

I smile at him. 'I will not give it to you, you know that, Ron,' my voice is steady, 'you will have to fight for it.'

'Ayya, tea?' Mary appears at the entrance to the living room.

'Yes, thank you, Mary.' Ron's public manners were always nice.

The food grows cold as Ron sips his tea. A blend of Assam

and Darjeeling—I can still make it the way he likes it. Tea making is taught early to girls in Assam. Ma showed me how when I turned six. First the utensils readied on a tray: the china teapot, although stainless steel is slowly gaining favour now, the tea strainer on its little bowl; the sugar bowl, the small milk jug and then the cups and saucers and the spoons for stirring. Then the making of the tea. The kettle brought to a boil—not for long or the tea would lose its taste—and the teapot first rinsed out with the hot water. Then the spooning of the tea leaves into the pot, one teaspoon for each cup to be made and one for the pot. Once that was done, the hot water was poured into the pot and the tea cosy placed firmly on it to keep it warm. Hot milk into the jug and a quick check to see there was enough sugar in the bowl and it was done. Just two minutes, that was all the time the tea leaves were allowed to brew in the pot, any more and the tea would be dark and bitter and lukewarm. Does she know how to make tea, this woman your father has fallen in love with?

The fried egg will be cold now, I can see its lacy edges curling up and hardening. The sausages sit congealing in their thickening fat. Even the toast will be too hard to eat. I am to be left with only the juice. Pointless to express indignation now; any gesture of censure will be met with your father's calm good sense. I never stopped you from eating, he would say, and that is so true, he has not, you see.

'You will have to give in, you do see that,' Ron's words are a statement of fact rather than a question.

I feel a racy thrill of delight. There are things that Ron does not see now; there is no need for me to submit to his will anymore.

'Nice seeing you,' I say, my voice bright with glee, as he rises to leave.

The rush of the confrontation ebbs just as quickly as it had swelled. The clutter of the breakfast things seem sad now, their very arrangement speaking of loss and of failure. Failure to be what they were supposed to be, incapable of reaching their goal now. Warm, vital things just moments ago, full of the promise of nourishment, they lie there cold, stale, unappetizing. I do not want them anymore; all I want is my bed. But I cannot go there in the morning, it is a place to seek out in crisis and I am not feeling desperate right now. Tired, overcome, but not desperate.

The bell rings. Second time this morning.

Mary brings me a packet. I hold it in my hands, it is light although the package is large. The brown paper is thick and when I run my palms over it I feel a soft yet tough layer underneath. It has come!

In a few minutes Mary has the breakfast things cleared, the table wiped and clean, all traces of the morning's encounter now gone. She hands me a knife with which I slit open the package. The bubbles of the wrap pop under my impatient fingers. I draw the sheaf of papers out carefully and lay them out one by one on the low table.

Preetha has not disappointed me: the drawings are more than I had expected. So she did see what I saw, her gaze was clear and confident. There, before me, is my book come to life.

You will love this, my darling, I cannot wait for you to see this, the story I have written. A book. A story of the forest that I have gone to over and over again all my life.

This was the one trip we made without fail every winter. My family and Joya's. We would all pile into Bipul Moha's black Ambassador, the men in front, the women and children at the back, and drive away, usually on a cold winter morning. The boot would be crammed tight with battered suitcases, cloth bags stuffed with packets of biscuits and larus and home-made cake, in case they ran out of food at the old Forest Lodge where we stayed.

Bipul Moha's stately speed of forty kilometres an hour coupled with the fact that we stopped every half an hour for either Ma and Bina Mahi to buy vegetables or fish from village folk squatting patiently by the highway meant that it was late afternoon by the time we arrived at Kaziranga.

By and large, Joya and I did well on this road trip. We would wheedle our way into the window seats and stick our noses out much like I see dogs doing now. My face and nose would soon grow numb in the stiff, chill wind but even then I would persist; there was so much to see and we stepped out of Guwahati so rarely. As the car trundled up the hills just outside the city I would feel an unexpected happiness surge through me. I still feel it, you will be surprised to know, every time I set off on a road trip. Something about leaving one's moorings behind on a quick impulse, no need to book tickets for a plane or train, just lock the front door and get into the car and go. What a relief to leave one's life behind.

Anyway, once we cleared the hills, still green then, not cut up and prone to landslides as they are today, we arrived at Jorabat, at the Crossroads, from where one branch of the road veered off into the dark, alluring hills of Meghalaya, the Land of the Clouds, and another turned left, climbed another hilly stretch and then descended with a sigh into the green valleys that would lead us to Kaziranga.

Of course, there was plenty to see before we got there: there were long stretches of countryside, some tame, planted with rice and winter vegetables, and then again there were wild sections where the forest crept up to the edge of the road. Wild birds, small animals were the treats that met our eyes here. We crossed the Kolong River at Nowgong, ran up a meandering stretch of highway lined by old Assam-type houses, some with old thatch roofs and stopped at Jokholabondha for a quick cup of tea. If we had dozed off before sometimes, we were wide awake now for Burapahar, the Old Hill, rose up from the flatlands before us a few kilometres away. We were almost there—the jungle was just a whisper away now.

As we ascended Burapahar Joya and I would be on alert; the jungle was closing in on around us stealthily. Sometimes we were rewarded by an elephant ambling through the brush in the undergrowth below the twisting road but very often it was only a hushed silence that met us. But even that silence was wild: it was a taut silence held up by the muted swishing of the trees in the wind, by the whirrings of unnamed insects in the distance. The call of invisible birds emphasized that muteness and we were silent too, under that familiar, much anticipated spell.

Once the road descended Burapahar, the forest opened up; patches of grassland now broke the monotony of the thick woods. This was rhino country and a few kilometres further on there was a swampy pocket they favoured, lying half-submerged in the dark waters as if relaxing in a pool. We would always see some there and even if we didn't we were not discouraged for we were sure to see many on the next morning's elephant ride.

Preetha has drawn Ganesh as if she has seen him firsthand. What is this uncanny power that she possesses? From my words she has distilled the essence of that beloved elephant and here he is looking at me with that mischievous look in his eyes. I thought I had finally achieved dominion over the nature of things by my delicate control over words, but Preetha has routed my skills; she has displayed so emphatically that a picture is enough.

jahnavi barua

Who is Ganesh, you must be wondering. He was one of the herd of domesticated elephants that the forest department kept for their use. The first time we met Ganesh, Joya and I were only six and the last time I saw him was when I visited Kaziranga with your father after our wedding. It was our honeymoon, I suppose, but no one called it that, it was considered too vulgar and since we were already so adept at the art of transfiguring we only said we were going on a trip. I was twenty-six then, your father, thirty and Ganesh was thirty too. Did you know that elephants live well into their seventies? That means Ganesh could still be at Kaziranga carrying people into the mist as the sun rises; I must take you to him one day.

Joya nominated Ganesh our official protector in the forests and grasslands of Kaziranga. I remember how afraid both of us had been when we were to climb onto his broad back that first time. It was dark, the sun had not yet risen, it was cold up there in that machan-like platform that was level with the elephant's back. The mist was disconcerting; it created the illusion of warmth, it was so much like smoke but when it touched you it was with a damp, limp hand. Shivering there, clinging to each other, we had refused to mount when Ganesh had edged closer to the landing and twisting his large head around touched Joya and me with his trunk. You will not believe it, but that was the most loving touch I had ever felt until that moment, not counting Joya's hard and sometimes painful embraces. And this softness undid me—I shook Joya's hand free and climbed awkwardly on to Ganesh's back.

Elephants are a wise lot; they can feel, think, remember and love, almost as well as human beings. Sometimes better, I would say. Ganesh loved me more than anyone else I have known, surpassing even Joya's love, for her love often had a hard edge to it, a darkness I did not care for. That same soft love overwhelms me now when I feel you within me. It is a round feeling, no hardness to it at all.

Ganesh is the hero of my story. When I began to write a year ago I wrote about him first—a story for children set in the grasslands and woodlands and marshes of Kaziranga. And although it was only a story every blade of grass in it seemed to me real; I felt I was telling a lie when I called my writing a story. How could I be sure it had not all happened a long time ago?

That morning as I rode on Ganesh's back, I was invincible. Nothing would ever frighten me again.

A long hot shower is good for the soul. But not so good for a pregnant woman, and it is certainly not the best for you. After I put Preetha's drawings away in my desk in your room I take a shower with the heat turned down to medium. Your father used to laugh at my showers; he said they were Turkish Baths and he was right for by the time I had finished the bathroom would be filled with a dense steam that made it difficult to see my hand at the end of my outstretched arm.

This morning there is little steam so that when I stand in front of the full length mirror and glance at it, I am startled. Shocked even. There is something not quite right about that image in the mirror. Then I see it: it is as if I have been redrawn with a darker ink than I had been before. The nipples are distinctly bigger surrounded by areolas darker than I ever remembered. And from the top of my pubic bone straight up to the navel is a line; the linea nigra, the dark line! My lower stomach swells up gently, soft with the extra fat and muscle I am laying on to shelter you. For the first time since you arrived I am exhibiting your presence. Soon, it will grow more and more difficult to conceal your existence. I begin to shiver. It is cold suddenly in this empty bathroom.

I cannot pretend any more—I *have* to confess, rid myself of this secret; for a brief terrified moment I believe that unless I tell someone else about you, I will lose all control and tell your father instead.

And a new yearning swells inside me; I want to be pampered and for you to be made much of. That is the right way, the traditional way to do things. I demand love. Now, especially now, *at least* now.

My fingers are trembling as I call Preetha. The phone rings for a long time. I am quite prepared for her not to answer. Very often she does not answer a call, that is one of the few things that unsettles me about her; she is busy, she has a child with Down's syndrome and she looks after him with a frightening determination but she directs that aggression to the outside world sometimes. It is to be understood that she may not take a call or even call back for she has important things to do. I am always apologetic when I ring and very often have to resort to devices like pretending I have an urgent message or matter to discuss and even then the impatience in her voice makes me stammer and hang up before I have said what I had set out to say.

Today I am too frantic to care. When she does not answer her cell phone I call on the land line. She answers promptly; her cell phone is charging, she explains.

'The pictures are great,' I say, even now concealing my real motive. 'Let's celebrate! How about coffee in the evening?'

Preetha is relaxed. 'Absolutely!' she replies. 'Five o'clock? Usual place?'

After lunch I cannot sleep. I lie down, on the wrong side, my right, I can feel the blood flow to you diminishing, but I am restless. For the first time since your father left, I am not sure of myself. He has spoken the word this morning. She must have put him up to it of, course, he must know it will never work but he has given way and crossed that last line. You can set it right in a matter of minutes. One phone call and your father would install himself back in his proper place but I will never feel secure again.

The sheer curtains are swept back by a gust of wind. The fountain grass is tossed about, its purple ears of seed whipping around like a cat's tail. Suddenly a chirping, *chwit chwit* and then that lovely bird, the male purple-rumped sunbird appears, balancing effortlessly on the swinging stalks. Another chirp and the green-brown female appears beside him. I watch them for a while and soon I am asleep.

The coffee shop around the corner is one of my favourite places. Although it is crowded and could do with a clean-up it has two redeeming features: it is a place I can safely walk to, thus being able to dispense with the services of Vincent, who sometimes looks at me reproachfully when I keep him waiting all day only to step out in the evening, and it has an unobstructed view of Richmond Road. I am not squeamish about looking at strangers—it is being stared at that I cannot bear.

Preetha has managed to capture a table upstairs, in the corner, by the time I walk in. I stop at the top of the stairs to look at her. She has pushed the chair back from the table and is sitting with her long legs splayed, a pose so masculine it is almost shocking when your gaze travels up and you see first the long hair, a curtain of black silk around her shoulders and then that sweet face with its high forehead, slim nose and a mouth that makes you want to trust her at first sight. This duality that Preetha possesses sometimes confounds me; her unmistakably female face and the hard strong masculine body with wide shoulders and narrow hips; her generous heart but her unyielding manner which can very quickly make you feel criticized, inadequate, deeply wanting in some basic way.

'Hey!' I ease myself into the seat across her.

'Hey, yourself!' Preetha's smile reveals her perfect teeth, little pearls glowing against her dark face.

The waiter materializes in seconds by our side: I order a lemon tea and Preetha a cappuccino.

'So, you are happy?' Preetha slowly stirs her coffee. She has a way of investing every thing she does with a languor that is infectious—I can feel the muscles at the back of my neck unclenching.

'Very,' I reply. 'Thank you so much.'

'So, what next?' Preetha is still fiddling with her coffee spoon.

'I guess the making of the book—editing and proofreading and more editing, you know how slow it all is.'

'All that will happen,' Preetha tosses her head, 'but what are your plans now? Another book?'

I take a deep breath. 'Actually, I have news. I am pregnant.'

Preetha's eyes widen. 'Wow! This is fabulous news. When did you know? How long has it been?'

'Over four months now,' I am smiling.

'My goodness, Ron must be so happy,' Preetha is smiling back.

'Um, well,' I look right at her, 'he has left me, sort of, for a while.'

Preetha's face is neutral. She drops her gaze, and comes up forward to rest her elbows on the table. I look away.

Outside, the road is clogged with cars, they move at a crawl and the exasperated drivers lean on their horns frequently. Thick glass separates us from the road; still, snatches of noise, although much attenuated, reach us.

This is the point where I should be allowed to break into tears but I know Preetha better than that. I look out at the road, at the slanting columns of sunlight falling onto it from the mesh of the overhanging rain trees and I sip my tea, thinking only of the astringent flavour of the lemon.

Preetha's hand creeps across the table and briefly touches mine. 'Who needs men anyway?' Her tone is neutral and I pick up from that and smile.

Women who had reliable men can say that with so little thought. I would not dare to be so careless.

You dominate the rest of the conversation. Preetha is full of advice, yet even as she gives it I can see her holding back. Tarun, her six-year old son, had been born with Down's syndrome and although nothing she had done had contributed to his being born with that she has never stopped blaming herself.

When I first met her, five years ago, Preetha had been prickly to the point of being offensive. She had been hurting then; it was impossible to know that without knowing her history yet she behaved as if the world owed her something for this tragedy that had so unexpectedly ruptured her life. She wheeled Tarun around in the park in a pram so fiercely that people, especially other women, turned away quickly from her. I found her sitting on the cement edge of the fountain in the centre of the park talking to Tarun, who was gurgling away in his pram. It was towards the end of my walk, I always ended up by the fountain where the air was cooler.

Preetha's voice had been so soft with love that my skin prickled. I must admit here that my first thought had been

jahnavi barua

one of envy; how magical to have someone of your own to love like that.

We fell into a conversation. She was a trained artist, who had begun illustrating books, working from home.

'I find working from the house easier now that I have to look after Tarun,' she explained.

Preetha lived with her husband, Sundar, and Tarun in a flat around the corner from the park. It was easy speaking with her, something that did not happen to me very often and I seized the chance. As the sun set and the shadows lengthened under the tall trees we stood up to leave. We arranged to meet the next evening again. And we did, falling into an easy pattern. Many weeks later she told me about Tarun but it made little difference to me; I did not pity her like the other women did. How could I when I was so much more wretched than she was?

A momentary concern had flitted across my mind this morning about Preetha's response to you—you see, now I was in a position of equality, no that is not the correct word, I suppose our positions were to be more balanced now. I no longer was worse off than she was but I see from her face that I need not have worried. Preetha has a very robust sense of fairness, sometimes too robust for she did not know how to temper it in accordance with circumstances.

Our cups are empty. It is time to go. Suddenly Preetha smiles. 'I tell you what,' she says, 'let's celebrate this properly. How about a road trip? Just women and children? You, me, Baby and Tarun?'

I am taken aback. 'I'll have to check with the doctor,' I say. Should I take the risk? I have been weighing risks all my life and am proficient at it but this time there is another life involved. I will leave it to Dr Joseph. And if she says it is okay, why not? I will go. You and I will go on this trip together.

Now that a chance has been given to me I am seized by an uncontrollable urge to get away from all that has become too familiar. Those trips to Kaziranga always left me feeling resurrected; this trip to a new forest may just do the same for us.

In any case, if nothing else, time would pass and you and I will have to wait just a little less longer for your father to find his way back to us.

four

Y ears ago, my mother had said that if I gave in to my baser instincts I would reap nothing but trouble. The way she said it, her lips compressed together, her eyes boring into mine, searching for signs of shiftiness, immediately provoked an intense feeling of guilt deep inside me. I was instantly and permanently convinced that there was something not quite savoury within me that I had to keep tamped down. It made me feel unclean all the time and I could hardly bear to meet Ma's eyes after that. The nuns at school only reinforced and perpetuated this burning feeling and I would blush if by accident I met someone's eye. Surely they could all see the darkness that lay dormant inside me. Some day I would be discovered for what I was.

So, when three weeks later Dr Joseph says confidently that she sees no reason why I should not go on a short trip as long as the road is good, the drive is short and I take adequate care, I am happy but the joy is shadowed by a familiar fear. This is a selfish thing I am setting out to do, gratifying myself without regard for you. Despite my eagerness I come home and I tell Preetha I cannot go. She will not accept that and calls Dr Joseph to reassure her that I would be taken care of.

Preetha's persistence wears me down; I relent and we plan our trip. We decide to drive to a resort on the Kabini River close to Nagarhole National Park. It is a three hour drive but Preetha is confident it will be an easy one.

'The jungle will be the perfect thing for us,' Preetha is emphatic.

We leave just as the sun rises on a Friday morning. Our departure is timed to avoid the heavy traffic that will build up later on Mysore Road.

As we speed down the highway, recently rebuilt so the surface is as smooth as a runway, I feel that old feeling of foreboding rise repeatedly within me. I push it down but as we leave the city behind us and are just cutting through the sprawl of industrial estates on its outskirts it rises so fiercely I almost gag.

'Preetha, stop!' I cry out and when she slows down and pulls over I yank my seat belt off and bolt out to throw up, again and again, on the grassy verge. I squat there, nose running, tears flooding my hot cheeks, yellow strings of vomit hanging from the corners of my mouth.

Preetha is behind me rubbing my back, handing me a bottle of mineral water but as I lean back slightly against her all I can think of is how afraid you must be feeling right now.

In the car I fall asleep mercifully, the seat belt holding you and me tightly.

When I wake up we are still in motion.

'Good morning, sleepyhead,' Preetha calls out cheerfully.

Tarun echoes her from behind. 'Good morning, Auntie Kaberi.'

I twist around to smile at the child in the back; he is sitting quietly, seat belt fastened for safety. He is such a sweet child; he has been given an extra portion of goodness to make up for everything else.

A signboard flashes by; we are almost halfway to Mysore. Have I really been sleeping for over an hour?

'Coffee stop?' Preetha glances at me.

'Sure.' I am feeling so much stronger now.

A familiar excitement is beginning to simmer inside me now. I look out. Rolling fields, different shades of green, slip past the window. It is so different from the countryside back home that I had been disoriented in the beginning.

Six years ago, Ron and I had driven to Mysore to spend a weekend away from Bangalore and I had been astonished at the landscape that met my eyes. It was all gently undulating land, very dry, I remember for that had been in February, covered by pockets of scrub mixed with just a few big trees. There were rocks too, small ones, big ones and some very large outcrops. Granite, Ron had said they were, they were granite stone. Stone was a treasure in my part of the world; very few in Assam could afford stone. We made do with bamboo; it was used for everything—for fences, walls, furniture and almost everything else. Stone felt so much more permanent.

Six years later, the landscape seems less rural somehow. Along the road are frequent clusters of shops, factory complexes, medical colleges—there seems to have been a building boom since I last passed by.

Preetha slows down and I see before us on the left a coffee shop. She turns into the gate and parks in the parking lot. I will be glad to see a bathroom and I am sure you will be too.

When I finish with the bathroom, Tarun and Preetha are already seated at a table. Tarun is eating a chocolate doughnut.

'With extra sauce!' He tells me as I approach. I smile at him. He has more sauce on his face than on his doughnut but with his faltering movements that is the best he can do.

We must have been an odd sight there; two women and a special child. No man with us. Not so strange if one knew

Preetha even a little; she did not need a man to prop up her sense of security. Sometimes it was even a little embarrassing the way she brushed Sundar off, as if he were a little schoolboy who had outstayed his welcome. I wonder what she had told him this time. Did he want to come on this trip and did she say 'Stay' like you would to a well-trained puppy?

Another hour and we cross Mysore. Preetha knows the roads well; she has grown up in Ooty, sorry Ootacamund, in the Nilgiri hills, her parents still live there and she has travelled this road often. Large chunks of her extended family lived in Bangalore so even when Preetha was a child they descended several times a year from their sky-scraping perch in the blue hills, on a road so winding and steep that on one section, the Sigur Ghat bit, there were thirty-six hairpin bends to negotiate.

Preetha said her sister would be sick all the way and there were times, either on account of the steepness of the road or because the road ran through protected wildlife reserves, her father would not stop and Vidya, her sister, would have to throw up in brown-paper sickness bags that their parents collected diligently from airplanes whenever they flew.

The car would be ripe with the odour of vomit when they finally rolled into Bangalore. It would immediately be packed off to the garage for a thorough wash while Vidya suffered at the hands of their aunt, their father's older sister, Lakshmi Auntie, who scrubbed her skin with the dried skeleton of a gourd until it sometimes bled.

'Did you not have the windows down?' I asked Preetha once. Our leisurely drives to Kaziranga with Joya and me by the rolled-down windows were never so fraught with tension.

'Oh no,' Preetha had laughed, 'Mum would not allow that. It would have ruined her blow-dried hair.'

This morning we have the windows down and as Preetha deftly makes her way across the outskirts of Mysore, smells of the city reach in to us: woodsmoke, then petrol fumes as we weave through some dense areas; finally, the clean air that races across the golf course as we finally make it to the outside of town.

Paddy fields and thick, dark orchards line the road now. Preetha speeds through them; after some time, is it an hour, I have lost track of time, we leave the main road going on to Ooty, turning right instead. The asphalted road is narrower here and it dips up and down more frequently now as the land suddenly shifts shape; it is more undulating and the gradient of the slopes steeper than before. The fields run up so close to the edge of the road it is almost uncomfortable; an unfamiliar tall grass, reaching over the head of a grown man, grows in clumps in these sloping fields cutting off the horizon and I feel hemmed in.

After about an hour the road bifurcates into two roads, both forks equally significant-looking. There is no sign; we can hear no sound of rushing water that could have led us to the river.

We are lost.

Preetha pulls over. She switches off the engine and all at once it is if we have entered a new world: one with that particular quality of silence I have almost forgotten. Sunshine splashes onto us through the windscreen. We are lost but unaccountably I am elated, happiness sweeping through me like a gale in April.

'Can you see anybody?' Preetha peers out through the windscreen.

'No.' There is no one. Preetha grunts and unbuckling her seat belt gets out of the car. I follow her.

We are parked on the top of a small rise. From here, now that we are above those small fields, we can see for miles around; the view is enchanting: the land rolls gently away, a sea of green, with an occasional sparkle of water—a stream, a pond?—in the hollows; the sky is a November sky, cloudless and blue. There is however no sign of human presence anywhere near us; in the distance an occasional wisp of smoke rising up into the air but too far to track down.

'Dammit,' Preetha mutters. 'Chalo, let's go.'

She starts the engine and then without any consultation, swings the car hard onto the left fork. I do not comment. The road meanders on: we pass the same fields, solitary banyan trees and, quite unexpectedly, come upon a hamlet. There are rough huts scattered along the road. A single shop, its wooden shelves lined with old tins, is open. A few men sit outside on a stone seat, under a scrawny mango tree.

Preetha slows down. She comes to a gentle stop. 'You stay,' she looks at me warningly. 'I will have to speak to them in Kannada.'

I make no reply.

Preetha is smiling as she climbs into the car. 'Onward! We are on the right track.'

Fifteen minutes later we are rewarded by the sound of water. It grows louder by the minute and then it is in front of us. A river, narrower than the ones I am used to, is to our right. Towards the centre of the windscreen is an enormous dam and to its left a lake born of that dammed river.

But something is not right; the road runs up to the edge of a small garden laid out at the foot of the enormous concrete structure and it widens into a circle and ends there. Apart from that patch of garden and concrete slabs with some words on it, no doubt commemorating the inauguration of the dam, there is no other structure in sight. Certainly no Kabini River Resort.

Preetha bangs the steering wheel. 'Where are we?' she yells.

At the back Tarun begins to whimper and in a flash Preetha cools down, she smiles and speaks slowly. 'It's okay. All under control. We will find our resort.'

'It must be on the right fork,' I say.

'Yes,' Preetha answers. After a pause she adds, 'You must be right.'

She turns the car around slowly. 'Look, Raja,' she tells Tarun, 'Look at all that water. It is the Kabini River.'

'Kabini,' Tarun echoes slowly.

We retrace our path. As we drive through the hamlet Preetha leans on the horn; she holds on for almost a minute.

At the fork we turn on to the other road. We follow it through an increasingly wild terrain. After twenty minutes or so, the tilled fields give way completely to scrubland and then the road abruptly joins another road at a right angle.

Preetha looks at me, her head tilted to one side. I look to my right; the bush along that side is reminiscent of jungle somehow while on the left I think the breeze is cooler.

'Left, I think,' I say.

We turn left and the car groans on the rutted track. I clutch at my stomach, holding it as well as I can. Preetha drives slowly, she has seen my concern.

Five minutes later, we are rewarded by the sight of water; on our right the trees peter out and we see the river again; it flows swiftly, its waters shimmering in the morning sun. I feel as if I have had a long, cool drink of water. I lie back and look up; on a telephone line to my left a white-breasted kingfisher sits patiently, its dark head cocked to one side.

An iron gate lies wide open ahead of us. We drive in and find ourselves in a concrete parking lot.

The resort has been laid out on a long, narrow strip of land bordering the river. We are at one end. A low, tile-roofed office building is to our right and from where we stand I can see similar low-rise stone-walled buildings rising one after the other, along the edge of the river. Narrow cobblestone paths run to and from these buildings connecting them.

'Well, we are going to be walking quite a bit,' Preetha says.

One of the boys unloading our bags has heard her. 'No, madam,' he smiles, 'we have buggies that will take you from place to place.'

Only now, when he has pointed it out, do we notice the golf-cart-like buggies parked on one side of the lot. But these will never do for you and me, little one, you will be bumped around too much.

Preetha and Tarun climb on to one of the buggies; Tarun is yelping with delight and Preetha has a hard time keeping him seated. I laugh at them and begin to walk to our cottage.

The first building I pass is the dining hall; a rustic wooden board, the words seemingly burnt into it, proclaims it so. After that the swimming pool comes into view—it is delectable. Really, it is—a long blue pool, deck chairs scattered around it invitingly. A ring of coconut trees holds the pool in a loose embrace.

The path meanders a little and by the time I arrive at our cottage, The Gulmohar, I am out of breath.

The door is open so I walk right in. A large room greets me. Two single beds joined together and another one under a window by the side. Towards the river, large glass doors open

jahnavi barua

out onto a pillared veranda. The river feels close enough to touch.

Tarun is already lying on his back on the joined beds. He is singing tunelessly.

'You don't mind, do you?' Preetha says gesturing at Tarun. 'I thought we could share?'

I am relieved, to tell you the truth. 'It's absolutely okay,' I say, dropping my handbag on the single bed near the window.

It is four o'clock. Preetha, Tarun and I are waiting at the small jetty to board the boat for the afternoon ride. In the morning, I had thought we would be too tired for this but after lunch we all agreed we were feeling fine enough for the boat ride.

The boat can seat around twelve people and here we are just the three of us. Are we too early? Tarun is growing restless; he is whimpering and Preetha is shushing him as best she can.

A small group of people are heading towards us now. Couple of boys in the resort uniform and seven or eight visitors. As they approach they all smile at us and one or two even say hello.

The life vests are muddy and stained; mine feels too bulky for me but we have to put them on. After a brief struggle we are all ready.

Preetha and Tarun are right in front on the starboard side; I am behind them. No one sits next to me and I am pleased. There is no need to engage in trivial conversation; I can focus on my surroundings instead.

The boat is now slowly leaving shore. As it picks up speed the distance between the marshy ground and the boat widens until we are riding in the centre of the river.

The leisurely pace of the boat, the water lapping at the hull, the breeze that runs its soft fingers across my face—they all conspire to soften my concentration. I could drift into a nap right here. But that would never do, would it? You and I would miss all the sights.

'Keep your eyes peeled,' Bipul Moha would tell Joya and me in the forest and that is exactly what I am going to do now.

Almost instantly, we are rewarded by a herd of spotted deer, the chital, knee-deep in water at the edge of the river, heads lowered, drinking. They raise their heads briefly as we pass but do not seem to pay us much mind.

'A Malabar pied hornbill, to your right,' Kumar, the guide calls out.'

Obediently we all raise our binoculars. I sweep from left to right and there, I see it. Sitting in the heart of a tree, very still, is the hornbill. It is large and the double bill gives it an impression of gravity, much like a justice in court.

The old fire begins to warm my belly. Can you feel the heat, little one? I am hunting again and all I want to see is the tiger.

'Are there crocodiles in the water?' From the way the man asking says water, I think he must be German. But I may be mistaken. So often I am.

'Yes,' Kumar straightens up to look at the man.

So, there is danger under even these alluring waters. I look away, aiming my binoculars at tree level to catch the birds. The guidebooks said there are over two hundred and fifty species of birds here—I want to see some of them.

At first, the trees seem homogenous, leaves layering more leaves, but then the eye adapts and I begin to see the birds. Some of them I know from Kaziranga and others from poring over Salim Ali's book: I recognize the rose-ringed parrots, the bulbuls, some barbets, the large green ones and the kingfishers that are everywhere. On the water, I can see the herons and egrets standing motionless while the pelicans sail away, oblivious to us passing.

'Elephants!' Tarun stands up, shaking with excitement. He is pointing to his right and there they are. A large herd—maybe ten—a couple of very young ones with them. They are playing in the water and while some of the older ones scrutinize us the younger ones are immersed in their play.

The boat has now travelled almost forty minutes. The sun is strong although we are in the shade of the boat's roof; the heat and the repetitive sounds of the water are again undermining my concentration. As if on cue, the boat slows down, then the skipper cuts the engine entirely; we bob silently on the steel-blue waters.

My companions are enthusiastic: they stalk the banks of the river with their binoculars, exclaiming over sightings, mostly birds and small animals. Preetha too is animatedly pointing out things to Tarun. I am alone in my soporific state. Just like I used to be on Ganesh's back in the Kaziranga grasslands—sleep opening its arms to me and I always willing to submit to its embrace.

Ten, maybe fifteen minutes later, the engine coughs into life again. We chug downstream and then I find the boat turning slowly in a wide arc; we are heading back to the jetty. The positions are now reversed—I am now on the outside, the boat is hugging the left bank and I have to look across the aisle to see. I shift a little to the left and scan the banks. The trees lining the shore are darker now and the shadows dense beneath them. Herds of deer dot the bank and I am now resigned to their monotonous presence. Then I spy it. At first I think my mind has conjured up its presence but someone else from behind exclaims in a sharp whisper. Tiger!

The mood in the boat changes instantly. People cross over to the left side, gathering in clusters but taking care to be silent. I look at Preetha—she has her hand warningly laid on Tarun's shoulders holding him down to prevent any sudden movements. I look over the shoulder of a burly German; I am cold with excitement, trembling. Can you feel it, darling? There is a tiger. Not more than twenty feet away there is a tiger on the river bank at the grass's edge.

The animal is a large one, its powerfully muscled body tense as it crouches at the water's edge, lapping at it. The boat is silent now again but he must have seen us for he raises his head again and again from the water. This is a shy animal, one reason why it is so difficult to spot—in all our years of travel to Kaziranga we must have seen a tiger only three or four times—and soon it gives up on its drinking and with a last backward glance in our direction, lopes away into the forest.

All of us return to our seats but the boat is silent. No one talks; we are imprisoned in our own thoughts. A tiger always seems to have this effect on people, robs one of all speech. It cuts us down to size, in a way, reminding us of our largely insignificant place on the immense stage of nature.

Tarun laughs and the spell is broken. All at once people begin to laugh and talk and it is a small celebration, there in the middle of the Kabini River.

The mood of celebration lingers on well into the evening. Preetha has unpacked her bottle of rum and sent for some Coca-Cola to mix the rum with. I am taken aback. Not by the fact that Preetha is drinking rum, but by her carrying a bottle. It seems such a masculine thing to do.

'We were lucky,' Preetha says from her cushioned cane chair on the veranda.

'Yes,' I say, 'it was lucky, spotting that tiger.'

Tarun joins in from the room. He is at a low table, riveted on a piece of paper. 'I am drawing a tiger,' he says.

'Lovely, darling,' Preetha answers without turning back.

A cold breeze drifts in from the river; it washes over us and my skin tingles. The river is a dark band now, we cannot see it but are more aware of it than in the daylight. The gentle lapping of the waters at the shore a constant reminder of its dark presence.

'Fabulous,' Preetha sighs. She is on to her second drink now; she is sitting with her feet up on a granite ledge and looks across at me. 'Great to leave one's life behind sometimes, na?'

I take a long drink of my orange juice. 'Heaven,' I reply.

Preetha is still looking at me, she turns her glass slowly around in her hands. She is making me nervous. The outside of the glass is wet with condensation. What if it were to slip?

'What next?' Preetha catches me unawares.

'What? What do you mean?' I touch my nose with my right index finger.

'Now that this book is on its way, what are your plans?' Preetha is impatient.

'Like I told you, it's not really done,' I am cautious.

'Ya, ya, but it is almost,' Preetha persists.

'Maybe you can write about Kabini, no?' Preetha waves towards the river.

'Why not?' Indeed, why not.

'What about Ron?'

I am angry suddenly. 'What about him?'

'What is going to happen? You may need to actually earn a living.'

I grip the arms of the chair. My voice is light. 'He'll come back. It's just a hiccup.'

'The seven-year itch?' Preetha laughs and I follow.

'What did Sundar say about you coming away like this?' I ask gently.

Preetha arches her shapely eyebrows. 'Not much,' she says. 'It is not unusual. We have clearly defined spaces.'

I do not answer. Space. Your father and I had very separate spaces too, only I did not want mine. I wanted always to give it up and immerse myself in the other.

A phone rings in the room. It is mine, but where have I left it? I rush into the room, following the strident ring. There, it is in my bag on the bed. I fumble in the crowded bag and find it.

Sonia again. I do not take the call. The phone rings for a while and then petulantly falls silent. Let me send her a message instead; less trouble than speaking with her.

I am out of town, I text.

A few seconds later, a neutral reply. *Wow,* she says, *on your own?*

With a friend, I answer. Then I relent—*and her son,* I add. That should do for now.

Preetha has poured herself a third drink. She catches me looking at her glass. 'Don't worry,' she laughs, 'we'll go for dinner after this one.'

I am stiff suddenly. 'Take your time,' I say. 'I would have joined you if not for . . .'

'Of course,' Preetha sits up. 'Hey, let's go, you need to eat early and turn in.'

We walk up the cobbled path towards the dining hall; it is lit up and a bonfire blazes in the small clearing in front of it.

C an one really leave one's life behind?

I have seen so many people desperately attempt that and fail so spectacularly that I have come to believe it is foolish to even try. The most pathetic failure right in my own home. My father, your grandfather, little one, has been running away from something all his life. What it was he sought so doggedly to escape was something I knew nothing of and cared even less about. What was and still is significant was the path he chose; he embraced drinking as his path to nirvana and how painful that path is, to anyone who has to walk it, is something I cannot describe.

The drink took my father away from us all—my mother, me, Bina Mahi, Bipul Moha—and put him beyond our reach. When I was small, very little, I remember my father merely as a presence that sat silently in the front veranda in an armchair in the darkest corner. As I grew he stayed there, never once crossing into the light to lift me up, to look at my face. He never found what he was looking for. If he had, would he not have come back to us?

I look across at Preetha and Tarun sleeping. There is a night light on—Tarun is afraid of the dark—and I can see

61

them clearly. Preetha is on her stomach, an arm flung over Tarun. The child is on his back, face peaceful in sleep. How far can Preetha run? Can she ever shut this innocent child out of her closely guarded space?

And I? How far do you think I can run?

As I lie on this single bed, by an unfamiliar river surrounded by forests I have never seen before, all around I hear familiar sounds: the lapping of water, the whirring of cicadas in the darkness, the occasional hoots of owls. My old life is right here beside me.

The curtains are open at my window. I look out. There are dark clouds passing across the face of the moon now. It will rain soon and even as I think it I can hear the sound of raindrops on the corrugated tin roof of the cottage. The pattering of rain on tin roofs, a sound that pulls me right into my life.

Moonlight spills into the room and in that silver light a ghostly procession shuffles slowly across it, disappearing through the glass doors into the river: my father first, his long hair falling across his wide forehead into his empty eyes—he looks at me but does not see me; my mother, diminutive but fierce, her white sador wrapped tightly around her shoulders, looks at me warningly, the lines between her eyebrows etched into a mark of Vishnu; she follows my father closely. Bina Mahi, her round face luminous in the light, smiles at me and Bipul Moha stops to wave; hand in hand, Joya and Bidyut walk lightly across and then—then your father appears. He stands by my bed, face inscrutable but still my heart leaps up, swollen with love.

I want him to hold me in his arms, the way he had that first night in Kaziranga.

Growing up, Joya had some absurd notions about sex. She acquired them in that out-of-control time, those four years of high school, just after we both turned thirteen. Not being in the least interested in reading, she came by her information, in haphazard fragments, from the most unexpected people.

One of her main sources of knowledge was Joymati, our resident thirty-year-old virgin, so most of the material we received was inherently flawed, Joymati having distorted and embellished some scrap of information she received until it was beyond belief. Joya's other sources were as unreliable: an older cousin in college, who believed that kissing a man could lead to a girl getting pregnant; then later on, biology textbooks that made the whole act between man and woman sound gruesome. I had no founts of knowledge to tap so had to depend on Joya, but somewhere, deep in my bones, I nursed a swelling feeling that Joya was mistaken, that we were missing something vital here.

In the final year of school, I managed to wheedle Ma into allowing me to join the local lending library and it was there that I received definite signals to that conclusion. A sudden paragraph in an otherwise insignificantly mushy book would be ablaze with passion; the heroine would be writhing in the throes of ecstasy in her lover's arms.

I remember, distinctly, the first time I read this out to Joya. We were sitting on my narrow, hard bed, our backs against the reed and plaster wall. Behind us, in the sitting room, the evening news streamed forth from the television. My father was sitting in his easy chair, glass in hand. The bulletin was full of bleak news, something we had reluctantly grown accustomed to in those turbulent years.

'Lies!' Joya cried out when we finished.

'How do you know?' I flared up, unexpectedly angry. 'How are you so sure you know everything?'

Joya had glared at me and then she fell back on the bed, limp and silent. This was her way of saying she would not engage in the conversation anymore. Her mind was firmly fixed on the truth as she saw it; she saw sex as repellent and even after she entered medical college and studied human anatomy and physiology in detail, the only emotion she could summon up at the thought of physical love between man and woman was pain. So, she endured her wedding night in silent agony and although she did not explicate, she did tell me in a hard voice that it had been as bad as she had expected. I did not ask for details nor did I ever know if later she ever found anything different in it. Some things are not spoken of, even between friends.

I am coming to the point of all this. Before I do, I must say that I am not sure I should be talking to you about all this. On the other hand, I would not want you to ever be as ignorant as I had been so I will allow you to listen to a few things, but when I ask you to shut your ears, you must.

The point I have arrived at is this: having been persuaded by Joya that sex was a miserable, painful thing to be borne with fortitude and courage for the sake of the marriage, I approached my wedding with the most unnecessary caution. I braced myself for this ordeal, armed myself with courage only to find myself disarmed on that sublime night in Kaziranga. But before that, you must be curious about the wedding, about how your father and I met and married. Listen, then.

A wedding led to a wedding, as it usually did in our remote part of the world.

In the middle of her internship at the medical college, on a hot steamy day in June, Joya finally got married. I say finally, for this came at the end of a prolonged, tumultuous period of courtship—affair, as they still say, in our small town—that had so upset Joya's parents that they had grown frantic with worry. Bina Mahi had become shrill with anger; there were endless rows in that house between mother and daughter and Bipul Moha, usually so exuberant, had grown silent and escaped every evening to our house to sit beside my father, accompanying him in his daily drinking. The tension even floated over to our house like a malevolent cloud; my mother's silences deepened noticeably and my father seemed to empty out his bottle at an alarmingly fast rate.

The root of the discord was Bidyut. The boy that Joya had unthinkingly fallen in love with was deemed unsuitable.

Even then, I possessed this capacity for being reasonable—a trait Joya found infuriating—and I found I empathized with Bina Mahi and Moha. When put down in black and white on a piece of paper Bidyut's credentials were far from desirable. He was one of the boys who hung around the corner tea shop—in fact, that was how the romance had sparked off. In our final year at school, when Joya and I walked home, Bidyut and a friend of his had taken to following us, teasing and heckling from a safe distance. Joya found his teasing amusing; she said Bidyut made her laugh and that was how she noticed him. Once her interest was aroused it was a small slippery slope she slid down before she fell violently in love with him.

Joya believed in free speech, free love, free everything, although only I knew that free love was something she advocated vocally but was too squeamish about to practise. Of course, people did not know that about her and soon the neighbourhood hissed and sizzled with the hot news of the romance that blazed between Bipul Mahanta's only daughter and Golap Das's good-for-nothing son.

Joya's little house erupted in flames; Bidyut's family was decent enough, they lived in the neighbourhood, simple middle-class people like us, but Bidyut! At twenty he had dropped out of college and apart from dabbling in local politics, spent all his time smoking—and maybe even drinking—at the local boys' club.

All this made little difference to Joya; she was going to study medicine and she would support both of them, if necessary, she declared. While her mother stormed and cried and her father cajoled and pleaded with her, Joya went brazenly around the neighbourhood with Bidyut. He picked her up every afternoon from the hospital on his battered Bullet and dropped her home, his motorbike throbbing insolently outside Joya's front gate. Soon after, as evening set in, Joya would walk out to the teashop to meet him and off they would go on their evening jaunt. Very often they sat at a Chinese restaurant near the Zoo where they drank endless green tea and stuffed themselves with oily noodles. Sometimes they went to an out-of-the-way spot on the river where they sat, backs against the dusty motorbike, holding hands. It hardly ever went further than that; I believed Joya when she said that for I knew how disagreeable she found sex, but the neighbourhood now judged her a bad character.

'Just once,' Joya said, one rare evening when we went for a walk along the Long Pond like we used to in the days before Bidyut, 'he kissed me.'

I waited for her to continue. Joya stopped and began to laugh.

'We were sitting on a rock right on top of Kamakhya Hill,' she resumed, 'the sun had set behind us, we could not see it, of course, but the river was, you know, beautiful.' Joya paused; she did not have too many words for beauty. 'Then he turned around and kissed me.'

'What was it like?' My stomach ached.

'Yucky, what else? Imagine someone else's tongue in your mouth,' Joya grimaced.

We walked on, a breeze blew in from the river which was less than a kilometre from us, and suddenly she said, 'He must really love me, poor chap.'

I had thought that same thing many times, naturally I did not say it out loud and I held my tongue now, but to put up with Joya's many eccentricities, you had to love her deeply. Like I did. As for her—I had never seen Joya so mellow before. She had always been exuberant, laughing suddenly, game for anything and she still laughed but there was a softness in her now that made her more aware of things outside of her. A beautiful sunset would never have caught her attention before. So, I saw her point too when she said she would not give up Bidyut.

Then there was Bidyut. It was not difficult to see why Joya had succumbed to him: he was tall and handsome in a certain way, with high cheekbones and a sensitive mouth—well, okay, a sexy mouth—and he took pains to build his body as most of our unoccupied, unemployed young men did. But more than that he possessed an insouciant charm that captivated women and made men uncomfortable. In time, Bina Mahi would yield to that same charm for all her initial opposition. Basically, Joya's falling in love was an ineluctable conclusion she had been powerless to resist.

An odd thing happened as I spent more time with Bidyut: there were occasions I found I caught a fleeting glimpse of something more in him than that smooth easy manner he so effortlessly projected. I thought I saw a strength of feeling beneath that dazzling surface that was at odds with what we all had known of him so far but I could never be sure for it was always so quick, that sudden flicker of an unfamiliar emotion.

Anyway, as I had begun to tell you, the wedding took place in June, the year Joya had commenced her internship. A gang of men had been at work for a week in her compound supervised mainly by my father for Bipul Moha was so overwrought he could do little more than dart around cracking his old tired jokes. The yard was cleared of all debris and then levelled and then finally the day before the joron a bamboo robha was erected and covered by colourful tarpaulin.

The day of the joron the morol had to be readied; Ma and I had been delegated this task, Jitu, a young cousin of Joya's assigned to us as an assistant.

We walked across to Joya's house just as day broke, the steel-grey light slowly turning white. The dew lay thick and heavy on the grass and drenched the bottom of my cotton mekhala; I didn't mind the wet ends clinging to my ankles, my thoughts were on the day, the moment, this spectral time when the world slept wrapped in the mist's cloudy embrace. Ma and I walked through the mist, parting it before us as if it were a gauzy veil.

The robha was silent, empty at this early hour, except for Jitu and another young man deputed to help Ma and me. It did not take us very long to complete the decorations for the morol; four young banana saplings, two feet high were planted at the corners of a rough square and then strings of auspicious mango leaves were strung between them again forming a square. On the bare ground, at one end of this cordoned-off area, Ma stood a large mirror, leaning it against a bamboo murha at the back. In front of this we marked off a smaller square on the ground with flowers and then filled it up with multicoloured flowers. Facing the mirror, a soft mat was placed; this was where Joya and her mother-in-law would sit during the joron ceremony.

jahnavi barua

I was excited as I finished the last bits of work around the morol; the joron ceremony was such a romantic one—I always thought so, even as a child. It was an ancient custom of paying a bride price, unique to these remote lands in the north-eastern corner of India—the parents of the groom attempted to soften the blow of taking a girl away from her parents; they tried, in a material way, to compensate for the loss and also I suppose, show how much they valued this girl-woman who would now grace their household.

The mother of the groom and other women from his family arrived bearing gifts of gold and silk. The bride was brought out to the morol to receive these women who would now form her new family. Once the mother of the groom arrived, she ceremonially placed the jewellery on the bride and draped the silk sadors around the girl's shoulders. This is where the mirror came in—the bride used it to look at her reflection to see the new ornaments she was being gifted.

The ceremony climaxed with the mother of the groom daubing the parting on the bride's head with the red sendur powder—the mark of a married woman—to the chorus of jubilant ululation of the women gathered around.

While Bidyut's mother, with moist eyes, anointed Joya with the sacred sendur, her best friend, Jeuti Bora, noticed me in the circle of young girls around Joya and instantly chose me as her son's bride.

The only emotion running through me the first time I was to meet your father was terror.

I suppose any young girl prodded into a marriage arranged by her parents would be apprehensive. In this case, I was paralysed by anxiety. You see, a wide and deep chasm stretched between your father's family and mine. While my family was solidly middle middle-class, my father a poorly paid schoolteacher, your father's family was a prosperous one.

Jeuti Bora, your father's mother, and my mother had grown up in the same middle class neighbourhood in Shillong and had even attended the same Assamese-medium girls' high school in Laban, but Jeuti had married well and my mother was nervous of her attitude now. Jeuti, with her fashionably cut short hair and diamonds in her ears, had after all, spent the last twenty-five years on various tea gardens around Assam, where her husband worked.

These tea gardens, enchanting oases of green calm, were frightening places to me. This was a world far removed from my humble one. Great wooden bungalows, some over a hundred years old, stood proudly in a sea of tea bushes, filled with polished teak and rosewood furniture and equally polished, shining people who, dressed in chiffons and silks, partook of strangely named meals—high tea, supper! And I, who had never had to wield a knife and fork ever, how would I cope there?

Joya added to my concern when she informed me that your father, Ranjit, had studied in an exclusive boarding school in Shillong run by Irish Catholic priests; what would I have in common with him?

In the end, my mother need not have worried. Mama, as I would later on call Jeuti Bora, took me in her arms and as I felt her heart beat against mine, I knew I was safe. Your father was cool and reserved. He accepted the plate of food my mother handed him but ate little. His father, your grandfather, tall, with a stern face, ate a lot and at the end of the tea had relaxed enough to laugh and induce my mother to laugh at his jokes.

Our wedding was fixed for the twenty-sixth of November. Those three days passed in a blur. All I remember was feeling uncomfortable all the time; my head was heavy with the bun pinned on to the back of my head and the pins used to secure it cut deep into my scalp; my silk riha-mekhela-sador was heavy and dragged me down. I was hungry for I had had to fast, I was thirsty yet I felt the urge to empty my bladder all the time. Later I wondered—did this initiation into discomfort portend the course married life would take in the future?

The wedding ceremony carried on late into the night, coming to an exhausted close in the early hours of the morning. In the course of it, I had had my hand tied symbolically to your father's and that was the first time I felt his touch on me. His palm was cool and dry; I was mortified that mine was damp with anxiety.

After the rites were over, I was taken to your father's paternal grandfather's house on the hill above the river. I remember sitting in the back seat of the car wedged between Ron and Joya. I gripped Joya's hand so hard she said there were tiny crescent-shaped cuts on her skin afterwards. In the grey light, the imposing mansion was illuminated with strings of coloured lights festooned all over it. I stepped over that threshold, was welcomed in as the daughter-in-law of the house and then returned to my parental home for a few more hours.

On my hard narrow virginal bed, I collapsed into exhausted sleep.

I threw rice over my shoulder as I left my father's home later that morning. I was giving my parents back the rice they had nourished me with all these years.

At the doorway, when I had bent to touch my father's feet he had briefly rested his hand on my head and I felt my heart swell up with an unaccustomed love. My mother's eyes were moist when I touched her rough feet, and when I turned to throw the rice I saw her face wet with tears.

In Ron's house the mood was festive. There was music playing and people laughing and I was bewildered by this throng of unknown people.

Mama and Joya took me to a room, decorated for your father and me. She told me that after lunch, your father and I were to set off to Kaziranga. I must tell you, the knowledge that I was to go a beloved place calmed me down.

We left in his father's new Honda City; I was dressed in a white silk mekhela sador as befits a new bride but Mama had packed salwar kameezes and jeans into my suitcase.

In the end, it was night when we turned into the driveway of the hotel in Kaziranga and after dinner and a shower, I changed into a pink nightie instead.

Intimacy was something I was hopeless with. That did not mean I did not desire it—I know there are people who are solitary and impatient with company but I was not one of them—in fact, I craved it with a hunger that was almost vulgar. Yet, I did not know the first thing about how to forge that personal bond with anyone. Everything I did seemed to push people away. The girls at school for instance; Joya, who was always at the centre of a large flock of girls, when she was not alone with me, would always seek me out at school—at lunchtime, or on the sports field—and she invariably had buzzing around her a swarm of acolytes but as soon as I entered their midst something changed. The buzz would stop, the girls would fall silent, one by one, all around there would be a palpable feeling of discomfort.

'It is because you are so silent!' Joya would accuse later.
'Well, so are Mala and Indrani!' I would retort.

'Yes, but they do not appear so distant . . . so, so disapproving!'

I would not admit it, but maybe Joya had roughly diagnosed the problem. I have seen it happen to others later. People so painfully shy, they appeared prickly and off-putting.

Joya and my closeness was different—it was the intimacy siblings shared where one did not worry about the deficiencies of the other; indeed, often did not see them at all. And now. Now I was here, in this snug room facing the most intimate situation of my life.

It was your father's coolness, his politeness that retrieved the situation that night: he waited patiently for me to finish with the bathroom and once he was done, turned off the lights with no comment. I had eased myself under the soft duvet by then and he slipped in beside me. His lips were dry and cool on mine and when I did not know to open my mouth he prompted me by firm pressure. I was always good at following cues and it wasn't too hard after that. Two thoughts ran through my mind that night: Joya had been absolutely wrong about this, and that finally I had someone to call my own.

I lie here now, looking at the patch of night sky visible from my windows, feeling an itching sense of impatience. Four months now since your father moved out and although I have tried to be patient, tried to be brave and all those things that Joya always went on about, I want your father to make up his mind now and come back. There is a worrisome thought at the edge of my mind; that somehow as time ticks by something will change, that we will both lose some opportunity which will never come back again. I will try to hang in here, this is

rebirth   73 an unchangeable fact, but somehow, I don't know how, things could slip out of control.

Preetha and Tarun are already dressed when I open my eyes. They are playing quietly on the veranda so as not to wake me. Seven-thirty, my wristwatch reads. Time to get up now.

At breakfast Preetha tells me she has decided to take it easy this morning. That suited me fine, I told her.

'Maybe I will swim,' she says, 'is that okay?'

'Fine.' I am carrying a swimsuit—a habit born of being with your father—and I can wear it now.

The coconut trees do not fully shade us from the sun but I do not mind. I do look up to check that there are nets put up under the coconuts; too many people I know have been victims of falling coconuts.

Preetha is stretched out on the striped beach towel, hands clasped behind her head. I examine her covertly from behind my big sunglasses. She looks more androgynous than ever in her single-piece swimsuit: shoulders wider than any woman's I have known, narrow hips, long muscled legs that she does not bother to wax, she has so little hair. Her chest would have inspired pity in high school but despite the unconventionality of her looks there is an instantly alluring quality about her. Maybe it is the powerful energy just visible under that languid exterior; even when she is lying down there one feels she could spring up like a tigress and dive into the water like a dolphin.

An excess of energy. That was one thing I had never possessed. On the other hand, I did things slowly, neatly and conserved my energy whenever possible. It showed in my body—although I had good enough tone and a flat enough stomach normally, the softness under the skin was plain to see. 'Everything about you is round,' Ron had once said and when I looked perplexed for I had an oval face and was tall and slim, he elaborated by saying that my arms and calves and breasts were all rounded. He did not say if he liked it and I did not ask him.

Preetha sits up suddenly in one swift motion. 'I need to go get some water. Will you watch Tarun?'

I look up at her. 'Sure,' I say.

Tarun is playing by the water's edge. He does not swim and so did not go into the water. Preetha said he had been hysterical the first time they had taken him into the water to try to teach him to swim and that they had all been so traumatized they had never attempted it again. I know exactly how he feels—I hate water myself and have never learnt swimming. Something about the loss of balance that first time when you launch yourself into the water is deeply terrifying to me.

Still, your father had insisted I buy myself some swimsuits and made sure I wore them around the poolside. 'Can't have you looking like your provincial self, can we?' he had said.

So, I have these colourful swimsuits that have never been wet save for when they were washed. This morning I have on one of my favourites; it is turquoise blue with a white trim and a halter neck.

I sit up to have a better view of Tarun. He is wheeling a car on the concrete apron around the pool. Suddenly, a yellow butterfly flutters into view above him. Tarun is distracted by the colourful thing and stands up, waving his arms at it. He begins to stumble after it. They are heading towards the water and even as I get up and begin to run I know I am too late and before I can grab him he dips as if walking down on to a step and with a splash drops into the blue water. The only thought I have at that moment is of you, but without any hesitation I jump right in.

The first shock is the coldness of the water. And then that moment of panic when the waters close over my head. But I know enough not to open my mouth. Miraculously, I can see Tarun thrashing about in the water in front of me and I reach for him blindly. As I draw him towards me I find I can crest the water if I stand on my toes and as I break water I see Preetha and other people running towards us. I feel someone grasp me from behind before I close my eyes and fall into darkness.

When I open my eyes again I am lying on my bed on a clean white towel that someone has laid out on the bedcover. A light duvet covers me but I am cold, so cold. The curtains are drawn against the glare and the room is filled with a green light. It is as if I am still underwater and for a moment I panic. Instantly Preetha is at my side.

'Are you okay, Kaberi? How are you feeling?' Her eyes are swollen as if she has been crying.

My chest heaves as I fail to contain my sorrow and all I can do is shake my head at her. I am sure I have lost you, you see, and that this is going to be my punishment.

Preetha balances awkwardly on the edge of my single bed. She leans over to hug me. 'Oh, don't, Kaberi, don't cry,' she says but all I can do is cry harder.

Preetha holds me until I stop; she sits up as I wipe my face and blow my nose.

'The geyser is on,' she says, 'I thought you may want to get out of that wet swimsuit.'

I lie down for a few minutes as she pads away softly to the joined single beds where Tarun and she sleep. When I shift I can see Tarun lying there, asleep.

I cannot feel you at all. Speak to me, darling, speak, *move*. Let me know you are there. I cannot feel you—how many times is it that you are supposed to move in a day—the kick count Dr Joseph had taught me. I cannot remember it now, I just cannot.

As I peel the blue swimsuit off myself and stand under the shower I stop shaking; the warmth of the water runneling down my back is like an embrace. I wrap my arms around myself.

The glass doors to the veranda are open when I step out dressed in jeans and a polo-neck jumper. Tarun is sitting on the hammock, swinging slowly. Preetha sits on a cane chair watching him intently. It is unsettling, this scrutiny; it has none of the relaxed innocence of a mother gazing upon a beloved child. This examination is, instead, very hard.

Preetha has heard me. She turns with a smile. 'Come, Kaberi, come sit here,' She holds out a hand.

I lower myself into the chair next to her.

'Hello, Kaberi Auntie,' Tarun's face is alight with a smile, 'I swam today!'

'Yes, darling,' I say. 'You were very brave.' I turn to Preetha. 'Is he okay?'

'Yes,' Preetha says. She leans across and grasps my hand. 'Thank you so much. Especially now.'

'No,' I stop her quickly, 'you would have done the same.' I do not want to talk about you. I want to wait and see what happens. And in any case, I am not absolutely sure Preetha understands. The only person who would understand now is your father, but we cannot tell him, can we?

It is in bed at night that I feel your first kick. Oh my child, you are still with me. But are you safe? Are you well?

I sleep badly that night and in the morning decide to forgo the safari into the forest.

Preetha tells me later that morning that they caught sight of a leopard crouching in the undergrowth barely twenty feet away from their vehicle. They filmed it for fifteen minutes and the leopard did not move at all; it watched them just as keenly as it was being watched.

This does not trigger any response in me as it normally would have. All I want to do is go home now.

It is almost evening when we set off. I have no interest in the scenery flashing past now; the perky music on the radio fails to revive me either.

We arrive at the outskirts of Bangalore just before nine; it is late but because of the lateness of the hour we have missed the endless, crawling traffic jams and in just over half an hour Preetha stops at my gate.

'Well, Kaberi,' Preetha says from her seat, 'take care, okay?'

I open the back door to lug my bag out. I stoop to give Tarun a kiss. 'Bye, you two.'

As soon as I open the door to the flat I know something is wrong. It is dark but there is a draught and I know the doors to the balcony are open.

My legs begin to tremble; I need to hold on to something. 'Where the hell have you been?' The familiar voice staunches my terror and I begin to cry.

But my mother was right. No one is forgiven his or her trespasses.

'And do you think you should be carrying that bag in your condition?' Ron's voice is hard with an anger that I can feel across the room.

There is a neat pile of bills on the coffee table next to Ron's glass. I know instantly what they are although I have never seen them before; I never had to, you see. Dr Joseph's bills were always sent directly to Ron's office every four months. And I never thought to stop them.

Silly, stupid me. Oh, how could I have been so careless?

'And when were you planning to tell me?' Ron's voice is rising now.

'Not here, Ron, please,' I sit forward on the edge of the chair. 'Everyone can hear.'

'Fine,' he says in that voice of stone and stands up abruptly.

I lean back but he bends across the table and hauls me up, his fingers closed tight around my upper arm. He hustles me into the bedroom and I know what is coming next as he tenses his arm.

I try to free my arm. 'No, Ron,' my voice is steady. 'Not now, with Baby.'

Ron clenches his fingers; I can feel the bruise forming already, the small capillaries popping and flooding the tissue with blood. It will blaze forth in rich colours tomorrow, but it is almost winter and I will be wearing long-sleeved jumpers.

Ron lets me go with a jerk and I lose my balance and sit down heavily on the bed. Hush, hush little one, it is only your father. You will grow accustomed to him in time.

_____

It is well past eight when I wake up and for a moment I panic. It is late, too late for your father's office bus. Then I relax.

Ron has obviously decided to take the day off. He is reading the morning papers in the balcony when I cross to the kitchen.

Mary is cooking up a feast for breakfast. She has pulled out the dosa batter from the fridge, one of your father's favourite breakfasts, and as she seamlessly ladles the creamy batter onto the hot tawa she has sausages grilling and oats bubbling on the gas.

We eat in silence but that is not so unusual for Ron never did say much in the mornings. Mary chats softly as she comes in and out, bearing hot, paper-crisp dosas for Ron.

Yet, as I stand at the kitchen sink scraping the plates out and stacking them in the sink, I see there is a tightness in her face.

'What is it, Mary? Everything okay at home?' I ask lightly.

Her back is to me but I have known Mary so long that I can see the hesitation as her shoulders tighten and then they relax and she answers in a voice from which the morning's effervescence has faded.

'It is that son of mine of mine again, madam,' she replies, continuing to cook. 'How I wish he had died in my womb!' she adds with uncharacteristic bitterness.

I am shocked. I lay my hands quickly on my abdomen. 'Mary! You know it is not his fault.'

Mary's first born, a beautiful baby boy, had developed schizophrenia as a young man of twenty; unusually early, the doctors said, something called hebephrenic schizophrenia— Ron had said that came from the Greek word, *Hebe*, for youth—that was particularly malevolent.

'I am sorry, madam,' Mary says, 'the illness is not his fault but he just won't take his medicines. Last one week he has not taken and now this morning he is hitting his father and younger brother and all the neighbours had to come and tie him up and take him back to hospital.'

Mary is crying now. She has turned the gas down; a dosa crackles softly on it while she wipes her eyes with the edge of her sari.

'Mary,' I say softly and put my hand on her shoulder. She grasps it briefly and turns to cook again.

Ron has settled back into the cane sofa on the balcony. I will have to find my own space today. Your room beckons. I sit in the straight-backed computer chair and look out of the windows.

The jacaranda is bare now, no feathery leaves to clothe its nakedness. Without its green cover it looks ugly; it does not possess a particularly appealing shape. But soon, as soon as the temperature begins to rise it will grow resplendent, confident, a different being entirely.

All this must be bewildering for you, little one. New voices and so much tension in mine. I haven't spent much time with you at all, have I? You must have grown. They say you are ten inches long now; that you are beginning to grow hair on your head and have eyebrows. Eyebrows!

Soon, I will have to prepare this room for you. There is a lot to do, child, before you come.

The computer is on this morning. It must have been Ron. If I am to be pushed in here I may as well check my mail.

Only two mails in my inbox. One from the clinic reminding me of my next appointment, two weeks away, and one from my editor saying she has received the couriered package of drawings. She also warns me that now editing will start shortly.

A spare and light inbox. Hardly anyone writes to me. My parents do not use the old computer they possess—they speak to me once a month, a conversation that does not shift in the slightest, so I know exactly what my mother will say; Ron's parents call very often, whenever they feel the urge and so do not need to mail. Preetha meets me every other day and Sonia calls. There is no one else really who is close enough to write.

Your father's inbox—now, that is always bursting at the seams. So many people write—I saw, once, as I was passing him on the computer, one thousand mails, one thousand! Of course, he had not checked his mail for around ten days at that point but even then—it would take a hundred people to write ten times for him to receive that many. Your father has many friends, I know that, but he does not introduce me to most of them.

Mary is standing at the door.

'What is it, Mary?' I think I know what she wants.

'I feel bad, madam, today Ayya is home,' she starts. It is true, Mary adores your father. 'But please, can I go home early?'

'Of course, Mary,' I shut down the computer. 'And wait.' I

cross into my room and find a five-hundred-rupee note. I fold this into her hand as she stands there with wet eyes.

By late morning your father retreats into the guest room. He has installed himself there; his clothes and other belongings he has cleverly unpacked in our bedroom. More subterfuge. But I can see that he intends to reside mainly in that cheerless spare room.

Music trickles out from under the door. Gerry Rafferty, singing about how much he loves his woman; an old favourite, but this morning the words resonate with me differently than they used to. Hollow and empty they sound to me.

Ron makes an appearance at lunch; we even sit down to lunch together and he eats steadily without saying a word again. Rasam and rice, the only other local dish he likes; apart from this he will eat only our Assamese food. I had to retrain Mary when she first started with us: first get her used to all our spices, many of them so different from the ones used here that she would be impossibly confused all the time; then to teach her how to heat the oil, temper it just so until it was smoking hot and only then toss in the seasoning and the things to fry and then finally, to teach her how to fry! That was so alien to her, to cook a vegetable merely by frying and not by adding water and boiling it. She learnt though and now we are not homesick for food anymore.

In the afternoon, I lie down but my mind keeps wandering off. I cannot stand this anymore; I decide to bake brownies. Tarun loves them and so does Preetha and then I have been so angry with Preetha in Kabini. I am not sure why and I hope she did not notice but the brownies will be the ideal sweetener.

That evening, at the park, by the fountain, the two of them, mother and son, plunge right into the box of brownies with dirty hands. Tarun gives me a big sloppy kiss on my face; I have to wash my face with water from the pool.

Preetha laughs. 'You are the best, Auntie Kaberi!'

When I let myself in, as quiet as a thief, into the flat, I find that the plate of brownies on the table has been attacked too. In spite of myself, I smile. See that, little one, I have not lost my touch.

This time I will not be let off so lightly though. When the knock comes on my door I am almost relieved.

Ron does not wait for me to reply; he walks in before I have time to settle myself. I have been lying down on my bed and I pull myself up into a sitting position, legs stretched out before me. The evenings have become quite chilly recently and I am not good with the cold; I am dressed in a thick fleece tracksuit and my feet are encased in thick woollen socks Bina Mahi had knitted for me.

There is a chair in the corner by the window but Ron sits down on the bed diagonally across me.

'We need to talk,' he says and I think this is so much like the soap operas on prime time television.

Of course, I know his first question.

'Why didn't you tell me?' Ron's face is impassive but I know what to look for.

His hands are balled into fists on his lap.

I have no answer that will satisfy him, it is all too complicated and so I do not reply.

Ron sits up straighter. 'Fine,' he says. 'Anyway, now you understand there is no question of a divorce.'

'Why not?' I am surprised.

'Don't you know why? Because of the child, of course.'

'Are you going to leave her?' My tone is more combative than I had intended.

'No,' Ron says, 'I will not. I will move back here, but I will come and go.'

Come and go indeed. My face is hot, my palms damp with sweat.

'That won't do,' I say, my voice stiff.

'What do you mean, *won't do*?' Ron raises an eyebrow but his sarcasm rolls easily over me.

'I mean exactly that. You are welcome to stay here, but not if you are still with her.'

'Who are you to tell me what to do?' Ron's voice is rising now but I am not afraid. I do not answer.

'And what will you do, what *can* you do, if I don't leave her?' Ron is mocking now.

The words just rush out of me, I am so angry. I am so sorry, child, I do not think of you or of Ron's mother, I do not perhaps even think of myself; later on I realize the risk I have taken but now I do not stop to assess that.

'I will divorce you then,' I say calmly.

Ron is incredulous. 'Divorce! *Divorce!* And how will you survive? Haven't you grown used to all this?' He points around the room, an actor in a play.

Your father underestimates me. I have grown accustomed to all the comforts he has provided me but I have not forgotten how to live with less.

But your father has not finished. 'And the baby? Who will give you custody when you cannot even support it?'

The breath catches in my throat. Custody? I had not thought of it. I grow sly with panic. 'Maybe they will Ron, with our history?'

Ron is furious. 'Are you threatening me? Don't *threaten*

me, you hear?' He gets up and I shift back. He turns and with quick furious steps is at the door.

I find more courage now. 'One month!' I shout at his receding back. 'One month, I give you to decide.'

Conflict affects me in a visceral way. I am miserable in a way that an unhappy animal is miserable: I no longer relish my food, I am constantly thirsty and my nerves are so tattered that I start at the slightest sound—the slamming of a car door, the shout of a child at play—and the slightest hint of criticism has me in floods of tears.

The other day I shocked myself—and Preetha—by beginning to weep at something she said. It wasn't anything remotely offensive; she had only pointed out, and rightly so, that if I did not take myself in hand, eat a little more and grow more cheerful, the baby would suffer. She had not known, when she said this, that Ron was back; she had merely commented on something that concerned her.

There we were, sitting on the rim of the fountain, the evening light gentle on our faces, watching Tarun turn round and round with his little arms spread out—he was a helicopter—when I began to cry. My face was wet with tears, my upper lip slippery with snot—Preetha slipped down and knelt in front of me in shocked confusion. I didn't have a tissue on me and I was mortified, so I covered my face with my hands.

'What is it, Kaberi?' Preetha was annoyed now.

'Ron is back.' My wail sounded pathetic to me.

'That's good isn't it?'

I shook my head.

'Well, why not?' Preetha was truly irritated now.

jahnavi barua

'He says he is not leaving her.'

Preetha was standing now, I could feel her looming over me, blocking out the light.

'When you cannot change something, Kaberi, you have to learn to accept it,' Preetha said in a flat tone.

'I know that,' I burst out, 'don't think I don't know that.'

Knowing that your father does not want to be with us, here in this flat, understanding now that he may leave forever, does not lessen the terrible ache inside me.

In the old days, before you, little one, I would wait all day for your father to come home from work. Now, it has all changed and I feel as if I am in a world where everything has become its exact opposite. Night has somehow taken over day and the day is as dark as the night; I cannot wait for your father to leave for work and grow frantic as the time for him to return draws near.

Not even when he is away am I at peace though; I am not comfortable in my own home anymore. All I yearn to do is sleep and I tell Mary I am not well—some sort of virus—and seek out my bed. Mary, distracted by her own troubles, does not probe deeper, content instead to nourish me with warm soups she makes from simmering mutton bones. So, I sleep, undisturbed, in my underwater room, unconscious of all that is happening around me. Sometimes, in my foggy sleep, I think I hear the sunbird calling but I cannot be sure and I do not care for it just now.

I take care to be up, washed and brushed and made up before your father arrives. There is no sense in pointless conflict.

In actual fact, we see little of each other. Your father enters my bedroom only to retrieve essential items; he is holed up in the guest room most of the time. He has stopped sitting in the balcony with his glass of rum—where is the time anyway? As soon as he has showered and dressed he steps out—of course, to her—telling me not to wait up and I don't. I don't exactly wait for him but I cannot sleep at night having exhausted my quota of sleep in the day. From my dark bedroom I can hear his key turn in the lock, his footsteps across the living room, sometimes crossing over into the kitchen, and then there are nights when I don't hear him at all. He does not come back at all; in the morning I tell Mary he had to go to Mysore for the night.

The last time I had to deal with sustained strife I had not fared much better than this while Joya, as expected, had flourished. Those had been the years of the Assam Agitation, when ordinary citizens led by young student leaders, still in college and school, had risen in peaceful protest against their own government. What provoked this unusual mass protest was the government's treacherous policy of aiding the influx of illegal migrants from a neighbouring country so that they could then vote for them.

It seems a distant dream now, darling, those turbulent years that have now receded into fading memory but our last seven years of school had been marked by this unrest.

I can still remember the excitement that swept through our neighbourhood when those first cries of protest were raised. It may sound insensitive, my calling this wave of emotion excitement, but right in the beginning it felt like that for us; here was an extraordinary diversion, an unexpected interlude that transported us out of the monotony of everyday life.

Andolan! Agitation. Revolution. It was Joya who first said that word to me; she had heard her parents discussing it. It was an andolan that was brewing: a struggle of the people, an attempt to breach the walls of government and express the will of a nation of people.

I was confused. 'Like the freedom struggle, you mean?' I asked Joya.

There was a glint in her eye. 'Exactly!' she said. 'Only this is not against the British but against our own government.'

You will never believe what happened over the next six years. It had seemed an improbable revolution when it commenced, but this storm brewing over our hills and valleys and rivers grew in strength and speed and focus until like the bordoisila that descended on us every April and swept away everything in sight, this revolution too swept clean all that stood in its path.

The leaders were unlikely ones: students, young men and women of the colleges across the state. In time their ranks swelled, as others—working men and women, housewives, old men, grandmothers, children—rushed in to join them.

'Good thing Ma is no longer with us,' my mother said, one morning, as we all stood at the gate waiting to join a group of neighbourhood women on their way to picket the Deputy Commissioner's office in Kachari Ghat. 'She would have jumped right in.' It was a joke and I smiled; I could almost see Aita leading the line of women, thumping her walking stick on the ground.

Joya's grandmother, Bipul Moha's eighty-year-old mother, did emerge from her house to fight for the revolution. One morning, Bipul Moha, who was a government engineer, in the State Electricity Board, came out of his house to go to work, only to find his mother at the head of a clutch of old ladies, blocking his way. They had come to prevent him going to work in a government office. The andolan had taken its lead in many ways from the Mahatma: it was a non-violent movement and civil disobedience, in an attempt to paralyse the state machinery, was its main path.

The exchange between Bipul Moha and his mother made us erupt in laughter.

Bipul Moha stood at the gate, his briefcase in hand. 'Ma,' he said gently, 'ask your young friends to step aside and allow me to go to work.'

'Can't!' Aita answered tartly. 'You cannot be allowed to go to work for a government that is betraying its people.'

'Ma,' Bipul Moha remonstrated. 'It was you who had asked me to work for this very Government, twenty years ago.'

Aita bristled with annoyance, 'Maybe,' she said nonchalantly. 'Times have changed.'

It ended with Bipul Moha defeated; he turned around and went back in.

The andolan was no laughing matter though; despite its non-violent methods the government hit back with force. Many died, others were wounded. Every time, the movement struck back with a peaceful strike, a picket or calls for state-wide blackouts, where no lights were lit in homes across the state. This seemingly mild form of attack did manage to disrupt completely the organisations of the state of Assam: huge oil fields in Upper Assam fell silent as workers could not work, the pipelines to the rest of the country dried up; tea production suffered; the people had managed to exert their will.

To tell you the truth, I enjoyed these blackouts: they were thrilling. All of us huddled into one room or sometimes we sat out in the veranda from where we could see the night sky studded with trembling stars. Old folks told stories, young ones listened. The violence and bloodshed seemed far way for a moment.

Joya became an active member of the movement. Although we had been only eleven when the andolan started it continued

jahnavi barua

for six years; by the time we were fourteen Joya had grown into a leader. She took the lead in our neighbourhood; whenever a picket line had to be assembled she would take charge; in the evenings, on blackout days she would roam the lanes of our neighbourhood with a gang of volunteers, checking that all the lights in every house were switched off.

I followed her when I had no choice, for instance, when we had to stand and picket an office or demonstrate outside the Legislature but I did not revel in it like Joya did. The sight of the armed police and paramilitary standing ranged before us, ready to strike when ordered, made me ill.

Joya was scornful. 'Coward,' she called me. Very often. And I did not attempt to defend myself.

'No love for your motherland,' Joya would berate me. That wasn't true. I did love this green land I stood on as much as she did, but everyone was not cut out to be a revolutionary.

My father stayed in the shadows; he approved of the movement, he made that clear but made no move to join it. On the other hand my mother plunged in fiercely and rose to the top; we saw her on television leading rallies, arguing with policemen. She would look at me dismissively when she came home and I hid my antacid tablets in my pencil box so she would not find them.

At the end of six years, the government conceded defeat; the Assam Accord was signed in Delhi where it was agreed foreigners would be identified and deported but what happened to that historic piece of paper is another story altogether.

Those turbulent times are almost forgotten now. But there is one incident that has stayed with me; it refuses to go away and it does not seem to lose its rawness as I travel in time away from it. Sometimes I think it grows more vivid as the years pass.

A hot suffocating afternoon in late August. The sky is heavy with glowering clouds that threaten rain. A demonstration has been planned; a procession is to march to Dispur to protest yet another student death in Upper Assam. A column of people have gathered in Judges Field and begin their march, in absolute peace, wending their way past the High Court and Digholipukhuri, the Long Pond before passing our way. Our neighbourhood contingent—Ma, Joya, Bidyut and I among them—join the now swelling mass of people at the Gauhati Club crossroads. For a while we are together, this familiar knot of people, and then the knot unravels and I find myself surrounded by strangers, men, women, children, all very friendly and calm. Many people are smiling and chatting and had it not been for the thin line of paramilitary Central Reserve Police Force on the edges of the road we could almost have been at a festive celebration; a subdued carnival.

As we walk on past familiar sights, the wet heat of the August afternoon grows more oppressive. At the Chandmari railway crossing, an oncoming train holds us up by more than ten minutes. The crowd is restive now, some younger children are crying and older ladies are seen leaving the main body of the column to stand or squat in the shade of trees and shop awnings. I am carrying a bottle of water and I drink from it and after I finish pass it to my neighbour, a young woman carrying a small child.

Joya had said to wear a mekhela and I had, excited by the exotic feel of the blouse tight against my breasts and of the air stroking my bare midriff. But now, the silk mekhela imprisons my legs in a film of sweat and I cannot breathe as my chest struggles to rise under the restraint of the unaccustomed blouse. There is a long way to walk yet, another six kilometres, at least; my spirits sink.

After the train has thundered past the level-crossing gates are opened and we cross, listlessly now, stumbling over the wooden sleepers on the railway track.

From the head of the column a cry sounds. *Joi ai Asom*! Long live Assam! The call is taken up by others and soon the people rally around it. I imagine I can hear Joya's voice shouting out in front, and then Bidyut's. I cannot see them but once again I can feel the electricity in the air.

Half an hour later we approach the Ganeshguri crossroads. Not long now to the seat of the government, the fortified area of Dispur. The crowd is charged now, people laughing again when suddenly the section in front comes to a halt.

'What is the matter?' someone whispers beside me.

An answering whisper. 'I don't know. Can't see anything.'

We could not see at first and then like a tidal wave crashing back we see the mass of people in front turning around and running back right into us.

'Run!' they cried. 'CRP lathicharge!'

But like an animal caught in a car's headlight I freeze there on the burning tarmac. Ahead I see a line of khaki surge towards me.

A woman in a cotton mekhela sador darts across the road pursued by a man in khaki. As I watch, mesmerized, I see his baton rise and fall on the head of the frantic woman. There is a crack like that of a coconut shattering and the slight woman crumples to the ground. A thin line of red appears at the nape of her head where it twists awkwardly on her thin neck.

Someone grabs at my arm and I scream and then I see it is Bidyut but I still scream; if I stop I will collapse right there on the melting asphalt. Bidyut runs pulling me and I run after him. We run headlong into a small lane and after we pass a few houses Bidyut stops abruptly and pulls me through one of the gates and into the compound of a small house. He drags me along the high wall of the house and then pushes me flat against the wall with his body. He presses hard obscuring my body with his own and as I listen to the sound of men in heavy boots running along the lane looking for us, I hear another sound— that of Bidyut's heart beating against mine.

I can never forget the acrid taste of fear in my mouth just as I cannot forget the hardness of Bidyut's body on mine. After the footsteps faded away, Bidyut releases me and then he does something odd. He takes my face in his hands and bends down to kiss me on my forehead.

And then, my darling, you know what I do? I close my eyes and then throw up, right there, on his white cotton shirt.

One evening—your father has been home for about a week now—I am sitting on the balcony. The last few days I have not been to the park, I am too tired I tell Preetha when she calls, and I am tired but the truth is I am feeling too wretched to make the effort. So, I sit in the balcony instead, to be able to look out at the ring of pink tabebuia trees and the children running around in the yellow evening light.

Your father comes home early from work. He disappears into his room but comes out soon after. He stands in the doorway leading into the balcony.

'We need to invite Sonia and Rahul for dinner. We owe them one. So, I have invited them on Saturday,' he says without any greeting.

But Saturday is just three days away. A swell of resentment

breaks over me. Look at me, I feel like screaming. Do I look like I can organize a dinner for your friends right now?

I look calmly at Ron. 'Okay,' I say.

This exchange of favours is the bedrock of Ron's relationship with the Kapoors; there is constantly an accounting going on. One dinner is returned by another. A game of golf is rewarded by a game of tennis. It is like a balance sheet both parties maintain and it is just as dry and unappetizing.

Sonia must be put out with me. I never did return that call she had made to Kabini, it was clear this time that I was fending her off. Now, of course, we would meet soon. Before that preparations have to be made, the campaign organized, so that the house and the food and I would meet Sonia and Ron's meticulous standards.

Paper and pencil in hand I walk around the house, taking stock. The windows are clean; Vincent had done them just before I left for Kabini, two weeks ago. The curtains, thankfully, have been washed too; that leaves the carpets and the rugs to vacuum, the upholstered sofas in the drawing room and the living area could use some vacuuming too. Ron had insisted that neutral, very pale fabrics be used in the formal areas to set off the carpets and rugs he and Mama had meticulously collected. The carpets are beautiful, in rich shades of red and burgundy and russet; there are Kashmiri carpets, a couple of Persian ones and one or two from Afghanistan. Ron's parents are enthusiastic and extravagant collectors and Ron has inherited this talent.

This multitude of beauty had overwhelmed me in the beginning. Ron's parents were living on a tea estate near Jorhat when we got married. The Manager's bungalow on the garden was an old wooden chung bungalow; a chung bungalow is a bungalow raised on pillars, wooden or otherwise, a very practical form of building, I soon realized.

The modest house that I grew up in would have fitted into the drawing and dining rooms of Ron's house. As I looked tentatively at my new surroundings an unforeseen realisation began to stir inside me; I saw with new eyes how very meagre my life had been so far. Don't misread this, child, I did not hanker after wealth or luxury or beautiful things; even at that moment sitting on plump sofas upholstered in soft velvet, eating at the art deco dining table polished to such a degree I could see myself eating every mouthful, I did not feel poor. I was not ashamed of my mother's curtains stitched lovingly at home out of printed casement cotton fabric costing all of twenty rupees a metre. What I felt was deprived—not of material riches but of what that wealth could buy.

Money cannot buy happiness; people are fond of saying that to make themselves feel better. I did agree with that but would like to make a small correction: money alone cannot buy happiness but money can, sometimes, sweeten the soil so that happiness is encouraged to grow. If my mother had not had to fret, all her life, over how to stretch the small sum of money my father gave her to run the household would she have been a more generous person? I cannot say with absolute certainty, but I do believe she would have been and my life would have been richer in many ways.

Mama, my mother-in-law, inducted me into luxury. She was a diligent, capable teacher and I was a perceptive student. To my astonishment, I had a positive aptitude for luxury. The different kinds of wood used to make furniture, the styles of furniture design; fabrics and their utility; colour composition of a room—I absorbed it all like a sponge and soon I outpaced even my teacher. While Ron and his mother still stood by teak wood and classical design, sometimes venturing into art deco, I had, in recent years, discovered an appetite for the contemporary.

jahnavi barua

Straight lines, minimal embellishment, the stark beauty of a flat chenille fabric seemed so much more appealing than the overwrought designs of before. But in our home, your father's will holds sway; instead of direct revolt I have achieved a compromise. The furniture and style is Ron's, but the colours and fabrics are mine.

The beige and vanilla fabrics in the drawing room we had both agreed upon—that had been when there had been no indication of a child on the horizon; now, my darling, I will have to work out an alternative scheme.

As I walk around from room to room, I feel better. My mother would have said, in an arch voice, *Work always makes you feel better.* Homespun wisdom, sometimes it actually works.

The bathrooms are gleaming but I will have to do a superficial cleaning on Saturday morning. Fresh towels—Ron will insist on the Shyam Ahuja ones—will have to be put out.

And flowers. Fresh flowers on every tabletop. I will buy the flowers from the shop across the park on Friday. Fragrant white lilies and red carnations that will resonate with the colours of the carpets.

Mary is pleased when she hears about the dinner; she is always happy to have people to feed. 'I will make my mutton chop,' she says immediately. I agree and then we decide on a menu of mutton chops, a coriander chicken, a black daal, masala brinjal and of course, fragrant ghee rice. I decide to cheat on the dessert; I will buy delicious sweet curd and serve it up with rosogollas.

Saturday night comes and the house is softly gleaming, the lamps lit and the fragrance of the lilies heavy in the air. I am in a black cotton mekhela sador, one of my favourites, and I feel unaccountably revitalized.

Sonia and Rahul arrive at eight, right on time. Sonia is in one of her trademark churidar kurtas—this one is black silk and diamonds hang heavy at her earlobes. Her sharp glance sweeps across the room—later on, I know she will scrutinize the bathroom, examine the labels on the towels and search the window sills for dust.

Ron is an excellent host; he fixes their drinks just right and says the appropriate things. Mary is admirable as she hands around the short eats on a tray, her face luminous in the soft light.

Sonia is laughing at something Ron is saying; I cannot hear them. They are sitting across me and I can only watch them as Ron leans towards her, flirting a little, his face soft and eyes animated. You would love to see him like this, darling, tender and laughing; I seldom get the chance these days. In the beginning, in those hopeful early days, he had been attentive, loving even. But those moments had petered off and an awkwardness grew between us. Maybe if you had come along sooner? But no, I should have been able to hold his love even without you.

The conversation flows; Rahul, who is sitting beside me, talks to me of the rising price of contemporary Indian art and I make the right responses, my mind half closed to this cosy scene.

Suddenly Ron is standing in the centre of the room, light glinting off the cut-glass tumbler of whisky in his hand. 'An announcement,' he says. My blood runs cold. He cannot be serious.

Raising the glass in his hand, Ron says quietly. 'Kaberi and I have something to tell you both.' He waits just the right fraction of time allowing Sonia to adjust herself on the sofa into an eagerly listening position. 'We are finally going to become a real family. Kaberi is carrying our little one.' He pauses again. 'And this is just between us for now.'

Sonia shrieks with delight and rushes across the carpet and plants a kiss on my cheek. Rahul shakes my hand, but I can see him looking at Ron, his gaze puzzled, confused. 'Ranjit Bora,' he says, 'you are a chupa rustum, man.'

Your father is a deep one, a fish of deep waters, as we say in Assamese. He has to have a clear motive for divulging this news this evening but I cannot, for the moment, see why.

The dinner is a success. Mary has been her consistent self and the food is delicious.

After a round of liqueurs, Rahul and Sonia go home.

'Good girl, Kaberi! I am so happy for you,' Sonia tells me as she kisses me goodnight. Does she really mean it, I wonder?

The dinner has unexpectedly raised my spirits. The white lilies in their heavy cut-glass vases lift my mood every time I pass them.

It may be my imagination but Ron seems to be spending more time at home these days. He does not go out so often anymore; in the evenings he ventures out to the balcony. We don't speak much but still there is a little more ease between us now.

Preetha is delighted to see me sitting on a bench in the park one evening.

'Hey! Welcome back,' she says and Tarun gives me a clumsy hug. Preetha pulls him back a little. 'Easy now, little man,' she says.

It is a release to be out among people again.

Preetha suddenly says, 'How about a movie? *101 Dalmations* is playing at PVR—shall we go tomorrow afternoon? Tarun is home from school.'

I want to go. 'Yes,' I say, 'that will be fun!'

Next afternoon I am at the door when Preetha messages, *Is everyone okay? Take a look at the television, NDTV news.*

An instant pain in my breast. I switch on the television in the living area.

Scenes of carnage—is it a riot, a bomb blast?—flash across the screen. I instantly press down on the remote button; turn the volume up. The scenes are familiar now, the trees are ones that I know, the houses with their corrugated tin roofs and half-timbered walls could only be in Assam.

The newsreader confirms it: there have been serial bomb blasts in Guwahati she says, in the capital of Assam. High-intensity bombs have exploded in six places around the city, several dead and countless injured. I begin to tremble, it is growing difficult to breathe. Under my warm sweater I begin to sweat. Run, I have to run, I have to run away. Just as I reach the front door, it opens and I run right into Ron's arms. He heard the news an hour ago and has rushed home to be by my side. He wraps his arms around me as I sag, my legs giving way below me.

He lifts me effortlessly, and I am heavy now with you, carries me to my bed.

'The news,' I begin.

Ron turns the television off and says to me in a steady voice, 'I know, I saw it. It's okay, Kaberi, relax now.'

He pours me a glass of water from the bottle on the dresser and I sit up to drink it, hands shaking.

I am trembling with fright. 'Call home,' I plead. 'Call everyone.'

Ron holds my arms gently. 'I have, Kaberi, I have. They are all okay.'

'I want to speak to them . . .,' my voice is shaking and I cannot stop it.

Ron dials my parents' number. The phone rings for only a few seconds and my mother is on the line. I cannot speak.

A rare December rain has fallen in the night. When I wake up in the morning it is still raining, a fine drizzle that blows in with the wind through my open window.

I roll over on my back. Something is wrong; I am still dressed in my trousers and sweater.

There is a dark bulk beside me on the other side of the bed. Ron? Has he been here beside me all night?

Trying not to wake him I ease myself out of bed. In the bathroom I am hotly self-conscious; I cannot bear to have him hear me in here.

Your father is awake when I emerge. An awkwardness is between us.

'Kaberi,' he says, 'I have fixed an appointment with Dr Joseph at ten this morning.'

I am glad he has. 'Thanks,' I reply.

Mama calls just as we are leaving for the clinic. 'Are you all right, child?' She asks. 'Did you sleep well?'

'How are things there?' I ask, in reply.

'Not good,' Mama's voice is tired. 'So many people dead. Many of them we knew, Papa and I.'

There is a silence.

'When will all this end?' I ask.

'Who knows?' Mama replies. 'Maybe never.'

The rain tree outside Dr Joseph's window has been washed clean by the rain; its leaves sparkle where the sunlight catches raindrops trapped on them.

Dr Joseph stands up as we come in; she leans over her desk to shake Ron's hand. Her voice is light and laughing. 'Finally, the perpetrator of the crime! Good to see you, young man.' She turns to me, her voice sombre. 'How have you been, sweetie?'

I smile at her. 'Not too good. I am sure Ranjit has told you.'

'Yes. Come.' She stands up and I follow her to the examination bed. I stand on the scales without prompting; I cannot see the numbers anymore and Dr Joseph does not tell me how much I weigh.

I climb up on to the bed and lie down; I untie the drawstring and push down the gathers of my salwar. I feel Dr Joseph's hand measuring from my pubis. The hand comes up and then stops; she measures again. Then, she asks me to stand up and measures my girth with a measuring tape. She has done it before so I am not surprised but she repeats the measurement this time.

I cannot read the doctor's face. 'Have you been eating well?' she finally asks when we sit down.

There is no point in concealing anything from her. 'No,' I say, 'I haven't been able to eat well at all.'

She writes something on her prescription pad, peels off a page and hands it to Ron.

'Some blood tests, the usual, and an ultrasound,' she says, 'but we won't do the ultrasound here. I want you to do it in St Peter's Hospital.'

As we leave the room, she calls your father back. I pass into the waiting room; the receptionist ushers me into the blood collection room where the white-coated technician draws a syringeful of blood. When I step out Ron is waiting by the receptionist.

'What is the ultrasound for?' I ask.

Ron smiles and steers me out of the room by my elbow. 'Just routine,' he says.

That same afternoon we are at St Peter's Hospital. It is crowded, the reception area is packed with people; the seats are all taken and there is hardly any standing room. Ron registers at the desk and then hurries me through to the Radiology Department but it is not much better there. There are people squashed together on the wooden benches and they line the walls of the passages, shoulders jostling shoulders. To add to the misery the passages are dark, there are no windows, no openings to the outside at all; the only break in the ochre-coloured walls are the doors that presumably lead into the rooms where the ultrasounds, X-rays and whatever else it is that they do here are carried out. You would never know it was only late afternoon in here; it is so dim it can pass off for night.

An acrid smell wafts out when one of the doors near me opens. It stuns me, this smell, and I can feel the bile rise in my throat.

I clutch at Ron. 'What is that smell?' I ask.

'What smell?' Ron looks around as if to look for the smell.

'Like smoke . . . no, like gunpowder,' I am sweating now.

Ron holds my hand. He smiles. 'Oh that. Just the solutions, I suppose, they use in here, you know, for the X-ray film and all that.'

I close my eyes; the smell fills my throat.

'Mrs Bohra?' A woman in a white coat is calling out my

name—mangled, of course, as it always is here—and Ron steers me towards her.

'Bora,' he says with a smile and the woman looks up sharply from her clipboard and then sees him. She smiles back. 'Sorry,' she says in a smiling voice.

Inside the room it is dark. Once my eyes adjust I see the room is as spare as it is dark: a single bed beside which the ultra sonogram apparatus is placed and a chair beside it.

The woman asks me to take off my sandals. She then leads me to the bed and helps me climb up. I loosen my salwar again and lie there with the kameez raised obscenely up to my breasts. The radiologist has not yet come but I am to wait in all readiness for her.

Ten minutes—it could be less but the minutes seem to last longer in hospitals—the door opens.

The woman in white is beaming. 'Yes, patient ready, Doctor,' she says.

I raise my chin to look. The doctor is a man; I feel cheated suddenly and then feel foolish for feeling that way. Why should I have assumed these things in the first place?

This doctor is a busy man; his hands are not gentle, they are not rough either, just matter-of-fact and I do not mind. I understand. I have been waiting outside.

We go through my history again—ours, yours and mine. I can sense your father watchful and listening; after all he does not know most of this.

As I talk the doctor is probing all the time, the firm pressure of the probe insistent against my warm skin. No one bothers to point you out to me this time. There is an urgency to this meeting that is beginning to unsettle me.

The doctor leaves me in no doubt. 'As you know,' he begins, 'there is something wrong.'

What could he mean? Something wrong? And your father knows about it?

Ron has drawn his chair closer to the doctor now. He looks at me; he is worried.

'It is something called Intra Uterine Growth Retardation or IUGR for short,' the doctor continues. 'Basically, what it means is that the foetus is not growing well. It is smaller than it should be for the time of gestation.'

There must be something wrong with my mind. I hear the doctor but I cannot fully understand him. The language he speaks, his choice of words, is so alien, so harsh, I feel as if he is talking about something else, someone else altogether.

He is explaining the causes of this IUGR now. It could be maternal malnutrition—am I malnourished? Or it could be increased blood pressure or some disease in the uterus they have not detected. Sometimes apparently it happens for no reason at all. Where does that leave us then?

After I climb down from the bed, thank the doctor with the distant eyes, we negotiate our way through the dim tunnel again. But in the bright afternoon light, brighter still as it reflects off the concrete parking lot, I am blinded momentarily.

I see you struggling to breathe. Hold on, darling, please hold on.

'I didn't want to upset you unless it was absolutely necessary,' Ron begins to say in the car, but I am not looking for explanations here. Or to enter into needless wrangling.

The fault, if there was any, lay within me. I burn with the certain knowledge that I had been heedless; that I had been sufficiently distracted to put you in danger. This is no time to think of myself—I will have to climb out of the mess I am in and attend to you.

I turn to Ron. 'Are we going to see Dr Joseph now?'

'Would you like to?' Ron's face is tired: the skin is dull and the lines tight around his mouth. Shorn of its customary wariness his face looks almost vulnerable. It occurs to me that it can't be easy for him now, not with two strong needs pulling at him from opposite directions.

'Yes, if possible.'

The sun is sinking slowly now; the tops of the trees are rimmed with gold while below, around us, it grows dimmer. The traffic is slow, it is the time that the evening rush builds up as people make their way home from work. Above us, in the golden sky, birds are wheeling home, some in large flocks, some in pairs, very few alone. As I watch them I can hear Ron talking to Dr Joseph.

'Thank you,' he is saying, 'we should be there in fifteen, maybe twenty minutes.'

Dr Joseph is gentle as she explains the situation to us. The preliminary blood reports have also come in now. 'Your haemoglobin is low, sweetie,' she says. 'That is the most likely cause of the IUGR.'

I make no comment.

'You must try and eat well,' Dr Joseph has assumed her usual professional manner. She spreads her hands out in front of her. 'You were doing so well, what happened?'

I still do not answer.

'Well, if there is anything bothering you, work it out. Ranjit is back now, so things will be okay.'

In the lift going up home I am seized by anger. 'Why don't you go back to her?' I ask Ron.

'Because I haven't decided yet,' he answers, an edge to his

voice. 'You gave me a month remember, I still have two weeks left of that.'

After Ron takes his things out of my bedroom after dinner, I lock the door against him.

There is a temple dedicated to the Nine Planets, the Nabagraha temple, on a hill called Chitrachal Hill in Guwahati. From our lane it is not too far away, a five-minute walk, and we would walk there often, Joya and I. It is an ancient temple and apparently, a powerful one; once upon a time this city had been renowned for its skill in astrology and people flocked here from distant corners of the subcontinent in pursuit of their futures.

Even now, those who believe that the movements of the planets and the interlinked patterns they create can determine the course their lives take make that pilgrimage to this mysterious temple and worship there. My mother and Bina Mahi would often offer prayers there: they went there to placate the planets every time my father drank more than usual; they went in search of success in Bipul Moha's career; they even went when Joya fell in love with Bidyut. I know Ma has been there to intercede on my behalf; she has prayed that my barren womb turn fertile and bear fruit.

Many of these intercessions remained unheeded—Joya married Bidyut and even died——but there have been concessions made. You are here, my darling, but I must admit I was always wary of that temple. It made me uneasy, absolute power always does. What if the nature of the power changed and a benevolent force took a dislike to you and turned malignant?

Joya and I trudged up the winding road to the top of that hill, not for the temple, but for the view from the top. Well, not right from the top, we avoided the temple with the swarms of monkeys that roamed all over it, but just a little below, on the side that faced the river. A narrow twisting lane led to an empty field—it must have belonged to someone, this plot, but it was vacant for the time being and convenient, being lushly carpeted with green grass and clover, and it had a majestic view of the Brahmaputra as it looped in a lazy curve from east to west.

There was a stillness in that spot that held me in thrall; it is only a superficial solution, I know, being physically removed from situations and objects and people that spark off distress, but however superficial, that small wedge of time and space allowed me to collect all the fragmented parts of me and although I could not put it all together perfectly, I still came down the hill in better shape than when I walked up it.

Those days, in our lives, there was no time or place to be alone: I was always surrounded by people—at home, in school, in college, on the street—there was nowhere I could be alone. Being alone was viewed with suspicion: was the girl growing moody, did this mean she was in love and planning to run away with a boy? No, being alone was not a good thing.

On that hilltop, the air scented by the voluptuous blossoms of temple trees, I was supremely alone. Joya would sit around for a while and then slide into sleep. I was alone there, the wind in my face and the river sparkling seductively at my feet.

I will remove myself now. As I lie in the dark, bedroom door locked securely against your father, I decide that I must remove myself from his path. For the time being.

So I lie in bed in the early mornings. I can hear your father around the house; he has never bothered with being silent anyway. When the front door shuts decisively behind him, I rise.

Mary resumes making her big breakfasts for me and although I don't have the appetite, I eat, forcing the food down my throat. I still seek out my bed, but that is permissible now that I have been asked to rest, but I try not to sleep; I read instead.

The book about the lost child ends on a note of hope: the child is not found but there is a reconciliation of sorts between the parents and it is discovered that the wife is now pregnant. A new life beckons.

Once I am through with the book I find I have nothing else to read and I visit the British Council Library in search of new ones; I return with a pile of books: short fiction, a novel and travelogues.

Propped up against pillows, I read. When I tire I look out onto my terrace garden. The sunbirds appear every day and a few other birds join them now and then. There is a bulbul who has become a regular visitor. He is a jaunty fellow; maybe it is his peaked cap that makes him so but he struts about so cheerfully he makes me smile. I can hear the parrots at play in the early mornings but they never come on to my veranda; I don't have any brilliantly coloured flowers to attract them.

Preetha calls every morning to check on me; I tell her I am doing well and it is true, I am so much better now.

'Why don't you start on the editing if you are up to it now?' she suggests one day. She is right, a few more weeks and I may be too tired and heavy to even sit at the computer. I make up my mind to call my editor.

Tara, my editor, is pleased to hear from me. We decide to begin work soon so we can work our way through the manuscript in a month.

I am careful to work only after your father leaves and I always wrap up my work before he comes; he does not know of my writing and I prefer to leave it that way.

My work now forces me to relinquish my bed; I sit every morning at the computer. This is a new challenge, for I wrote my stories longhand, sitting at the dining table. The computer is unfamiliar to me and I fear it just as I fear something unknown. What if I hit a key and something terrible happened? If everything was deleted or if the computer crashed? I had this image of the monitor falling off the table and breaking into ugly plastic pieces whenever I thought of it.

Preetha holds my hand securely and soon I am able to sit and work without too much anxiety. As I lose myself in the stories again, the anxieties all recede into the background.

As the sun sets, I shut down the computer in a hurry and arrange myself in my bed, surrounded by my books. When your father peers in I am absorbed in my reading. He stops to chat a little every evening; he enquires about my day and I give him the expected answers. He is relieved, I can see, that I have stepped back from the line of conflict.

One evening—a week has passed since the hospital visit—your father does something completely out of character: he brings me a big bunch of flowers—fragrant white lilies, oriental hybrid lilies—and stands by my bed holding them awkwardly; he has never brought me flowers before and he does not know how to give them to me.

'They are lovely,' I say, struggling not to laugh, 'the vases are in the sideboard, on the left, you can choose what you like.'

In the end, it is I who am surprised. Your father has arranged the heavy stalks gracefully in the cut-glass vase; he places them on the chest of drawers and in the next few days I find my gaze returning to them again and again.

After he carefully deposits the vase on the glass top of the dresser, Ron stands on the rug in front of it, looking at the arrangement.

'Do you remember,' he said, 'how the mali would bring in cut flowers every morning to Mama? Buckets of them! I loved watching her arrange them.'

I feel a twinge of unexpected sadness. 'Yes,' I say, 'I do.'

Can you smell the fragrance of the lilies, little one? I don't know why but after a few days their cloying scent begins to unsettle me.

Tara and I forge an immediate bond. I am wary, at first, I always am, I do not expect to make friends easily and then Preetha has also warned me not to expect the editors and others at the publishers to be my friends. 'Separate the professional from the personal,' she had said.

Despite my caution I cannot help but respond to Tara; she is enthusiastic about my writing and she is not feigning it, I know, for she points out my strengths and weaknesses with unnerving accuracy. Sometime, it is almost intrusive, the skill with which she can roam my mind; but I soon relax, for she does it with infinite gentleness and courtesy.

One day, she says something that I do not expect. 'I miss home when I read your stories.' Tara is from Bengal and we share a common landscape; she says the description of the forest takes her back home. In Delhi, she misses the voluptuousness of our fecund land.

I could have easily agreed and said that I too missed home but something stops me. An uncertainty wells up inside me: what is this place that I should rightfully call home? The bond with the land I was created from is unmistakable but there are other ties that bind me to this new land now. How can I relinquish the claim this adopted land has on me? I have built a home here; your father and I have been happy in it, once upon a time; I have found you here; I have grown to know the trees and the birds. Surely, I am bound by these unshakeable links.

Tara's comment sets off a tumult inside me. I plead ill health and withdraw from my work. I make my way back to my reading but I am distracted; a restlessness has seized me within.

Your father has noticed the change. 'You seem a little down these days,' he says as he sets the tray with my supper on it on the bed. He has taken to warming up dinner and bringing it to me in bed; we are finally using the wooden tray I had bought for those romantic breakfasts in bed. 'Why don't you come out and eat with me?'

After a few evenings I do come out to the living area. Ron plumps up the cushions behind my back and brings me a footstool. He also has a surprise: he has cooked his mother's yoghurt chicken. One of my favourites too and he knows it. In the early days he used to make it often, every Sunday was doi-chicken day. We watch a travel show and I am surprised but I sleep well at night.

We eat together every evening now. Having company stimulates me to eat better and some nights I am positively ravenous.

When Dr Joseph weighs me a week later, she exclaims with delight. 'Fabulous, Kaberi! We can safely say we are back on track.'

The evening of the doctor's visit your father has a proposal for me. 'Why don't we start doing up Baby's room? I have a slack period at work. What do you say?'

Your room. I have not spent much time in it recently, but Ron is right, this is the time to start decorating.

'Yes,' I agree. 'Yes, this is a good time to start.' Another ten days and the year will draw to a close. A silly, sentimental notion, but I would like your room to be ready by the New Year.

And while your father is here, I could use the help.

We have not talked about your father's decision lately. Just once when he was telling me about happenings at the office he stopped, checking himself, and I knew instantly he was going to say something about her.

I was cruel. 'Have you told her about Baby?' I ask.

Your father flushes. 'No,' he says. And again loudly, 'No and no one else either except Rahul and Sonia.'

'What about Mama and Papa?' I have been worrying about this.

He shakes his head. So. He has left all his options open too.

'I haven't either,' I say. 'Not my parents. But I have told Preetha.'

He does not react. I am lucky.

The weather has shifted while I have been indoors. It is cold outside and windy. All along the roads, in the gutters at the edges, lie piles of dry leaves, plastic wrappers and other unsavoury debris. They lie still only when the wind dies down for a moment and then swirl up again, pushing ahead a little and coming to a rest when the wind quietens.

I wrap up warmly; besides my warm sweater I put on a

jacket and a muffler when I venture out with Ron in our quest for things for your room. The groundwork I did earlier speeds up our search immensely; Ron is pleased that we do not have to wander around aimlessly.

The cot is already ordered—I have also ordered a changing table to match it; I ring Mr Sen of Good Designs to ask him to deliver it. It arrives one Saturday morning; I remember well the disputes your father and I had had about the finish of the wood and I watch warily as the delivery men unpack it.

The men place the cot against the wall under the northern window. I feel a surge of pleasure as they settle it; I had been right about the knotty pine—it looks so warm and cosy. Your father is standing beside it, arms crossed over his chest. He looks thoughtful. I am beginning to worry when he smiles. He looks across at me. 'Looks good,' he says.

It is time now to tell Mary—foolish to think she will not notice the cot and wonder. If she hasn't already—I have been wearing loose clothes and am not showing as much as many other women I have seen; maybe Mary thinks I am finally putting on that long-needed weight.

Ron leaves the room to pay the delivery men and I take the chance to call Mary in. She comes in from the kitchen wiping her hands on the apron she wore over her sari.

She smiles. 'You called, madam?'

'Yes.' I smile back. 'I have something to tell you.' Mary's eyes stray to the baby cot; she is puzzled. 'A baby is coming soon, Mary. Our Baby!'

Mary's hand flies to her mouth. 'Ayyo!' she says, 'Sorry, madam, sorry!' She comes up to me and extends her right hand. Her eyes are shining. 'I am so happy, madam, wish you and Ayya all the best.'

As I take the rough hand she clasps our joined hands with her left one. 'Madam, you should have told me, madam, I would have looked after you; and here I am, foolish woman, telling you about my troubles, my son and suchlike. I would never have told you such things!'

'Thank you, Mary,' I say.

Now that your cot is here it is easy to put the other pieces together: Ron orders the mattress from Springwell and then we attend to the soft furnishings.

One Sunday, we head out to The Nursery in Ulsoor.

'Yellow,' Ron says, when the girl in the shop asks us what colours we are looking for.

'No, blue,' I counter. 'Only blue.'

Ron's face tightens. 'Isn't it better to choose a neutral colour?' His voice is reasonable; he is making an effort, he does not want to frighten the girl.

'I like blue,' my voice is light in response.

'But what if—you know?' Ron's tone is even gentler.

I smile.

'That is a risk we will have to take.'

By the end of the morning we are done: cot sheets, bumper for the cot, receiving blankets for you, even the baby bag has been ordered—all in shades of patterned blue fabrics. Blue animals walk all over the soft fabric; the forest is making its way into our home.

There is more to be done. A mountain of things to get ready: your clothes, my maternity clothes, but now I know I will have them done in time.

It rains again that evening and Ron and I decide to have hot soup for dinner.

The news is on the television and we are watching it desultorily when without warning I am filled with a strange longing.

'Come to the bedroom for a minute,' I tell your father, 'there is something I have to show you.'

The thick brown packet is where I have laid it down carefully—in the bottom drawer of my bedside table.

Your father is standing by the bed on the rag rug. I sit down on the bed facing him and with scrupulous care draw out the precious film. The bedside lamp is on and I raise the black and white film so it is placed before it.

Your father squats so he can see better. With tender authority I trace you out for him.

My finger is running along your spine. 'See that? Those are the vertebrae, all curled up together.'

Your father's finger follows mine faithfully.

'And there's the foot,' he says, his voice quiet and still.

'Yes, and look here, here are the eyes, the orbits and further down . . . there, those dark spaces—those are the lungs, the heart . . .'

His long fingers caress every image, dark and light, and then he lays the film down on the bed. I slip it into its cover.

Your father is still in front of me, on his haunches. I reach out and take his hand in mine. My face is hot but my mind ice-cool. His hand is limp and obedient in mine and I draw it closer and very carefully lay it on my stomach. Place it on you. There, little one, this is your father.

As if in response, you kick. Your father's face is red. Without moving his hand he moves to sit down beside me. I raise my sweater so now his hand is on my skin. Again you kick; I can feel his skin burning into mine.

Very slowly your father leans towards me and I do not move; I do not resist. His cool lips touch my hot ones and I allow him to push me down gently.

Even in the dark, his skin knows mine and I allow myself to relax and let go. The warm waves close over me this night.

For the first time, little one, I am weaving dreams for us.

As I fill the shelves in your cupboard with miniature blue clothes, my heart is singing. So many things to look forward to now. We will take you to the seaside, I can see you there, fat legs wedged in the sand, the foam on the water tickling your skin.

You can ride on top of Ganesh, the king of the elephants in Kaziranga; we can roam the forest together. Be strong, child, grow and rest, not very long now and we will meet.

There is something we can do now, your father and I, we can introduce you to the family.

'Mama and Papa first?' Ron asks and I agree.

Even as he is speaking on the phone, I can hear Ron's mother's squeals; when he hands the phone to me she is so overwrought I hardly have a chance to speak.

'Why haven't you told us till now? Are you eating well? Do you want me to come down and help?' She stops to take a breath and continues, 'Is it a boy or a girl? Oh, how silly of me, they are not allowed to tell you these days, but I hope it is a girl. Oh, you sweet thing, thank you so much!'

I smile. 'I am fine, Mama,' I say, 'Baby is doing well too.'

'Do you want me to come?' she is quieter now.

'If you can come when Baby is due,' I say, 'that will be a great help.'

'I will absolutely be there.'

Mama's enthusiasm is heady. When I call my mother I am feeling strong.

Ma listens silently as I speak. 'Why haven't you told us for so long?' she finally says. 'Is everything all right?'

'Yes, of course,' I am curt. 'What could be wrong?'

'I don't know,' Ma counters. 'You tell me.'

'Well, things are fine, surprisingly,' I am angry now.

Ma softens. 'This is good news, Kaberi. Jeuti and Amrit must be very happy, no?'

'They are, Ma,' I say, 'and you? And Deuta?'

'Wait,' Ma says, 'talk to your father.'

'Well, Majoni,' my father's slow voice is in my ears. 'I have been listening to your mother. Let me say, I am very happy. For all of us.' He pauses. 'Our blessings are with you.'

'Thank you, Deuta,' I say. 'I will be in touch.'

One call left to make. Bina Mahi and Bipul Moha are delighted.

'Hey, girl! Finally, I get the chance to be a Koka,' Bipul Moha chuckles.

One Saturday morning, I notice that the plants in the veranda are drooping and listless. I feel a pang of guilt—I have been so absorbed in other things I haven't even given them a thought this past month. The manure and *Trichoderma* packets have not even been opened.

Ron is standing at the veranda railings looking out at the park.

'May I ask Vincent to come up and help with the plants?' I ask.

'Sure,' he says.

Vincent and I mix the kilogram of *Trichoderma* with five kilograms of organic manure. This should be enough for all the pots and there should be a good bit left over for the next time.

From the sack filled with the rich dark mixture I spoon a little into each flowerpot and mix it in with the soil.

'There,' I say aloud to the plants. 'A little bit of goodness for you all.'

The ficus are shedding leaves as is the frangipani in the corner. Winter is upon us and no one can fight it. The climbing jasmine in the corner is still flowering although less vigorously then before. I resolve to send a few sprigs to old Mrs Murthy across the landing. She is always happy to have them.

The fountain grass is dry and straggly. It needs to be cut, to be headed back. The birds will have to do without breakfast for a while. I hate to do it but only after a deep trimming will new, healthy growth establish itself again.

'We had a pair of purple-rumped sunbirds here,' I tell your father.

'Great! Maybe they will nest here in the spring.' Ron smiles at me.

'Why don't you invite Preetha and her husband for a meal?' Ron says. I am not sure I have heard him right.

'What did you say?' I stop and look at him.

Ron twists around and repeats himself. 'I said, why don't we call Preetha and Sundar over?'

'Sure, if you want to.' I am taken aback but I don't show it. Your father does not like Preetha. Among other things he has called her 'subversive'. He thinks she is too strident for a woman.

The plants are done. I wash carefully, especially under my nails. Can't risk any infection now.

On an impulse I switch the computer on—I want to check my mail. As it comes on, I wonder why Ron has suggested this. But maybe there is no reason at all, just a desire to be sociable.

Two mails waiting for me in the inbox. One will be from Tara, she has been gently impatient with me these last two weeks; she cannot understand why I broke off work when we had settled into a rhythm. How can I tell her about the things I have been weathering?

I click on the inbox icon. Yes, I was right, one of the mails is from Tara. But the other! I feel a surge of pleasure; it is from Bidyut. This is a real surprise, Bidyut did not keep in touch with people; after Joya's death he drifted away from the family, keeping in touch only sporadically with Bina Mahi and Bipul Moha. Bidyut's withdrawal opened him up to attack in our small circle. Where, in the natural course of things, he would have been an object of pity and run the risk of being suffocated by pity and cosseting, he was now judged arrogant and hard-hearted. You see, child, he did not suffer in public and that is something you are not easily forgiven.

Bina Mahi and Bipul Moha took a slightly different stance; they did not think him insensitive, they knew him well, they knew he suffered. Their complaint was that he had pushed them away. They were more than willing to be there for him; after all, they had all lost the same precious person and now he was all they had to remember her by. They had misread Bidyut; he was not willing to become anyone's mascot, all he wanted was a measure of space to grieve alone. He realized soon that he was going to be denied even this and he withdrew. In his absence, Joya's parents grew increasingly bitter about him, often regretting the fact they had allowed Joya to marry him, but I really couldn't see the connection there to her horrific death.

We lost touch along the way. I called Bidyut a few times after Joya died but his monosyllabic answers made me nervous and then he never made any effort to keep in touch. Besides, your father and Bidyut had never liked each other; now that distance made it easier for all of us to drift away.

Still, I would have liked to have had some contact—he was the only remnant of Joya I had left too. And I had always liked him; he was so naturally charming and I had always thought he had liked me too. We had been quite a threesome; after all, every time Joya and Bidyut fought, and that was quite often, they both ran to me, and I had to soothe their inflamed tempers and sort out the matter between them.

In fact, Bidyut and I had been close; he was the one good friend I had apart from Joya. With him it was sometimes easier than being with Joya; he seemed to not only understand me as well as Joya did but he was effortlessly accepting of the way I was. No hard edges here; Bidyut had a way of holding my hand, he would stroke my fingers with his thumb slowly as he held onto them, that melted my heart. It had hurt when he withdrew from me but I decided, early on, not to take notice of this wound. It would not do to encourage it to grow.

Yes, little one, I would have been happy to have had Bidyut in our lives. Things may have been different with him around.

On and off, I tracked him. I had heard that he had a big falling-out with the political party he had aligned himself with after the andolan. The same student leaders that led the andolan had formed a political party and entered electoral politics; they won a resounding victory and Bidyut, who had enrolled in the party, had been a key worker. But somewhere along the way, this same party had gone the way of all political ones and embraced corruption—Bidyut left the party at this point. He tried his hand at various ventures and I had heard lately that he had launched—literally—a floating restaurant that was docked on the riverfront. I hear he is doing well.

Has he heard about you, child? Is that why he has mailed?

No, he does not seem to have heard of you. His mail is short and precise; he says he has been meaning to write but has been busy. Now he has an email account—I can hear the laughter in his voice—and so he thought he would inaugurate it by writing to me. I swell with pleasure; I am happy that he wrote to me before anyone else.

In return, I send him my love. I do not tell him about you yet; but I promise to keep in touch.

Tara's mail is cautiously admonishing; we need to finish editing soon, she repeats. I am feeling benevolent this morning. I tell her we will start work now.

On Sunday, the day Preetha and Sundar are to come, I am relaxed. No worry that Preetha will run her fingers along the tabletops to check on the quality of my dusting. But I do not forget to get flowers; lots of red and orange gerberas. Tarun loves bright flowers. Mary has made Mama's Khao Suey for tonight. I know everyone will love it.

Ron is dressed in a dark-blue kurta and loose churidar tonight. I too am in a red kurta and salwar—the most comfortable thing these days.

When the bell rings, your father rushes to answer it; I am sitting in the balcony. I rise to greet them all and as I walk into the light I see Ron kissing Preetha. He then moves around to shake Sundar's hand and then he bends down to Tarun's level. His face is tilted down so the other two do not see him but as Ron looks at Tarun I see an odd expression on it. Then I have it; it is an expression of distaste, of disgust at what he is confronted with and my heart lurches in fear. But Ron has collected himself and the evening progresses wonderfully.

Sundar, who is a shy man, opens up to Ron as he discusses his work with him—he teaches Physics at a national institute here. Preetha and I are kept busy running after Tarun, who is more distracted than usual. The night ends on a note of unforeseen warmth. I laugh, as I undress for bed, thinking of Tarun sucking on the noodles at the table.

e i g h t

The end of the year is upon us. Another four days and the
tired old year will disappear and along with it will vanish
old regrets, lingering sorrows, unfinished tasks and all the
other detritus that life dredges up. This is a hope—no, a
belief—I subscribe to, in full earnestness. That focused
thought seems to always ensure that the new year is what it
should be: a sparkling new start, the beginning of good things
and a chance to change over.

This year is no different. I feel buoyant as the days slip
past. Good things are happening; I can feel it in my bones that
even better times are ahead. With my heightened awareness I
can see that others can feel that electric tingle too.

Preetha and Sundar are driving up to Ooty to spend the
holidays with Preetha's parents. They ask us along; Sundar
seems to have taken a liking to Ron. Preetha sells Ooty and
its winter charms persuasively.

'It is cold, I have to admit,' she begins as we amble around
the park, 'but it is a fresh kind of cold, you know, the kind
that makes you want to dash out and climb a hill. And then
there is Christmas—it is a big thing there, the old churches
are decorated and so many parties, plum pudding and punch
and all that stuff, you will love it.'

I know it will be lovely. The old pines creaking in the wind and fires crackling in sooty fireplaces. There is no question this year, of course.

'Thanks so much,' I puff just a little, 'we would have loved it. But no more car travel. It is too late for that.'

'Next year,' Ron says, when I tell him of the invitation. 'I have a lot of friends from the gardens there.'

So, it will be next Christmas, with you, my darling.

Ron has made other plans for the New Year. There is to be a party at Sonia and Rahul's and he has promised to be there. 'Should be fun,' he said to me. Sonia's parties were legendary; Ron will have a good time and if I feel too tired he can drop me home and go back again.

'Make sure you don't stay too late,' Mama calls to warn.

'Do you have to go at all?' Ma questions.

There is good reason to stay back; even Sonia will understand but Ron has been so looking forward to this night that I cannot bring myself to hide behind you and refuse.

Soon, the last evening of the year arrives.

Ron helps with the clasp of my diamond necklace; as it sits sparkling on my collar bones he lightly runs his fingers along it. It is a truly beautiful sight. To set it off, I have decided to wear my black pat mekhela sador with the silver zari work. Black is your father's favourite colour and I have grown accustomed to it now. In our part of the world, in Assam, this is deemed an inauspicious colour, one that is malevolent and no one would think to wear black, especially on happy occasions. Until recently, one could not buy a black mekhela sador in the shops; Mama had to especially order this one at the weavers. But I hear things have changed so much, even back home, that it is not taboo anymore to wear black.

Sonia and Rahul live in Koramangala, roughly eight kilometres away from us. They live in a house, not a flat, a fact they were constantly emphasizing; it made flat dwellers like me feel positively second class.

The house is on a small rise and as we turn into their street I can see it blazing with lights. It is like a ship lit up at night on a dark sea. The street is clogged with cars; there is no place to park and Ron drops me off at the gate. He will try and find a parking space on the next street.

'Go in,' he says, 'it is cold. Do not wait for me.'

But I disobey, shivering outside in my thin silk outfit, the wind reaching in and teasing me with cold fingers.

'Why are you waiting outside?' Ron grips my elbow as he rushes in through the gate. 'Come in quick.'

The heavy teak doors open and we are greeted by a burst of noise: there is music playing, some sort of pop music with an insistent beat, but even that cannot hold its own above the clamour all around. People are talking everywhere, a drone fractured intermittently by a peal of laughter or a good-natured shout. The French windows of the drawing room are flung open but even that does not soften the din—all it does is carry fragments of conversation back into the drawing room.

Soft light from scattered lamps illuminate the fine room; the glow cast from them like luminous veils that shift with the flow of wind and sound. For a moment, I feel giddy and step back, onto the hem of my mekhela. Very quickly Ron's hand is at the small of my back—a steady, warning support.

'Darling!' Sonia is in front of me. She bends to kiss me briefly. 'Lovely, lovely to have you here. Make yourself at home. Drink? No, how silly of me . . . here Ron, look after her, will you?'

As she glides away, Ron smiles at me and winks. 'We are already a little happy,' he says and I laugh.

We walk together, arms linked, Ron and I, navigating around the bits of furniture strewn around the large room; I can feel his hip brush against mine as we move closer to avoid a peg table or an armchair.

A waiter leans towards Ron and appears a few minutes later with a glass on a tray. Ron gently untangles my arm from his and takes it.

We stand in a corner, near a console table with pink roses on it. I smile at Ron and look around. There are so few faces that I recognize but I can see Ron smiling at many, raising his glass in greeting.

After a while Ron turns to me. 'Want to sit down?' he leans in, speaking into my ear to be heard.

I am grateful. 'Yes,' I whisper back in his ear, 'maybe outside.'

There is a chair vacant near a charcoal fire—there are many lit in iron braziers against the cold—and I sit down. Ron pushes his way through the crowd to get me a juice. He returns red in the face. 'A real crush,' he says, 'it is crazy.'

I turn the glass around in my hand. Ron stands beside for a while, hailing passers-by and chatting with them. He looks down intermittently, smiling, but I can see in the strain of the smile that he is growing impatient.

'Why don't you go and circulate?' I say. 'I will be fine.'

'Are you sure? I can stay,' Ron squeezes my shoulder.

I tap his hand.

'Go!' I say lightly.

After your father leaves, I pull my sador over my shoulders and chest. It is too cold to brave an attempt at fashion.

'Hello, Kaberi!' Rahul, stout and gallant, comes up to my chair and bending down takes my hand.

'Hello, Rahul,' I pull my hand out gently.

'Is everything okay? Have a drink?' Rahul makes a game of looking down for my glass.

I raise it to him. A spark from the coal fire catches a facet of it and it glints like a diamond.

'Wonderful!' Rahul says, 'I like to see the girls happy.'

He walks away to enquire after his other guests.

I am burning hot on the side of the fire while on the other I am frozen.

'Do you mind . . . may I?' A skinny woman in a black dress drags a chair to the fire; I wince as I imagine the grass tufts being ripped up underneath.

'Not at all,' I smile at the woman.

'God, it's cold,' the woman warms her hands over the fire, leaning dangerously close to it. She is in a backless halter; I would be surprised if she felt warm.

The woman looks up at me; her face is lit up softly by the fire. 'Hi,' she says, 'I am Radhika.'

'Hello.' I smile. 'I am Kaberi.'

'Bengali?'

'No,' I reply. 'Assamese.'

'Oh,' Radhika says rubbing her palms along her bare shoulders. 'I thought Kaberi with the B and not like V, in the south here.'

'I know,' I am soothing, 'many people think that here.'

'Is that an Assamese sari you are wearing?'

'Yes,' I say, looking down at my sador, 'only it is not a sari, it is a mekhela-sador.'

'Really?' the woman looks across curiously, 'what is that?'

'Well,' I try to think of a suitable analogy, 'it is like your half-skirt here. No, it is more like a sarong that we wear as the skirt and then a second piece of cloth draped on top.'

'Ah,' the girl smiles, 'like a Burmese longyi.'

'Exactly,' I smile back. 'Like the longyi it is stitched so it is like a tube skirt that you have to step into.'

'You know,' Radhika leans conspiratorially towards me. I am afraid a spark from the fire will scorch her. 'I have always been fascinated by the North-East; it seems so dark and mysterious. Tell me, what is it really like?'

I laugh. 'It is certainly not dark although some bits are beautifully mysterious.' I tell her a bit about our land at the tip of this vast country; how it is wedged between it and several others—Bangladesh, China, Burma—and how because it has been at this crossroads forever the people, the food, the dress, the culture of all these regions have blended together and over the centuries been distilled into a unique potion.

'For example,' I say, to illustrate this point, 'for the six hundred years before British rule we were ruled by Shan kings from Burma.'

'Really,' Radhika's pupils are wide open in the firelight.

'Yes, really,' I laugh, 'and they spoke a language similar to the Thai one since they were kin to the Thai people and even today some of these Shan descendants—they are known as Ahoms today—speak it.'

I can almost predict what Radhika will say next. 'But you don't look Assamese, you know, chinky eyes and all that.'

'Well, all Assamese don't look like that although a large section does, the ones stemming from Tibeto-Burman and other Mongoloid stock. Some of us migrated from the northern plains of India centuries ago.'

'What about the troubles now, you know, the insurgents and all that?'

I don't know what to say. 'Well, they are weakening now. But they are there.' I do not pursue the topic; it is impossible to explain to an outsider how feelings of alienation have flared into a malignant blaze.

'Awesome,' Radhika's eyes are glazed now. She is switching off and I am thankful.

A waiter is bearing down on us with snacks on a platter. 'Hungry?' I ask and we flag him down and persuade him to put his plate down beside us. We proceed to finish the plate; there are salmon rolls, chicken tikka kababs and batter fried prawns. Are you full now, little one? I hadn't realized I was so hungry.

Radhika stands up to leave; she comes around the fire, a little unsteady as the heels of her stilettos sink into the ground. She bends down to kiss me on the cheek. 'Lovely meeting you, Kaberi,' she says. A whiff of tikka wafts across my face. 'Same here, Radhika,' I smile up at her.

My strays, Ron called them, these strangers I ended up having intimate conversations with at parties.

Eleven o'clock now. My back is hurting, I long to lie down, to get away from this crowd. Above us the sky is cool and dark; the stars shiver in it.

I notice the terrace above the main house. An idea forms like a bubble in my head. The air must be fresh there and there is no sign of any one. I rise from my chair and wrapping my sador around myself tighter push my way through the throng of people.

Inside the house the air is dense with the mingled scents of perfume, sweat, cigarette smoke and alcohol. My stomach churns. I make my way to the lobby and from there ascend the curving staircase to the upper level.

The small landing at the top is lit up brightly. A door is set into the wall on the left—that must lead into the terrace. I turn the handle down and open it cautiously. I stand still in the doorway, adjusting to the darkness outside. As my gaze travels across the still expanse I catch sight of something unexpected. To my left, just beyond the wedge of light thrown out from the landing, a man and a woman are locked in an embrace. I watch transfixed as the dark profile of the man bends down to the woman and meets it in a kiss. I am paralysed, too embarrassed to move away.

'What the hell?' the man looks up and in the same motion steps back, unwisely, into the light.

My blood runs cold. For a moment all I can hear is the roaring of the sea in my ears. It is Ron.

I turn to flee. I raise the hem of my mekhela to free my legs and I race down the stairs. I stand there, in the lobby, hugging the wall. I cup my hands around my stomach. You are all I have now, my love.

An angel appears before me. It is Rahul. He is flushed from the heat of the party; there are two points of red on his cheekbones.

'Kaberi,' he says in that slow voice of his, 'are you okay?'

'Actually, no, I am not feeling too well,' I say. 'Can you drop me home?'

Rahul insists on seeing me into the house. I step into the lobby and we smile at each other across the door.

'Thank you so much,' I say.

Rahul bends to kiss me on the cheek.

'Not at all,' he says, touching my cheek with his hand. 'And a very happy new year to you, Kaberi.'

'To you too, Rahul.'

I undress slowly in my room. The diamonds I lock up

securely in my cupboard. I drape the black silk across the back of a chair. I brush my teeth without looking into the mirror. If I see the face Ron looked at I will cry.

I lie down, cold, so cold. And wait.

Half an hour later, more or less, I hear the front door open. Then the knock on the door. 'Kaberi, are you awake? Open up.'

I seal my ears off with my hands.

He knocks again and again and again. I am trembling now, I cannot bear it.

Another knock and I rush out of bed and fling the door open. I charge at him and slap him hard across the face. He is shocked and automatically slaps me hard back. I am sobbing now, great tearing sobs. I swing out at him again and again. He moves back as I push forward.

'How could you?' I wail. 'When you said it was over.'

He is fending off my flailing arms.

'I never said anything.' His voice rises. 'I never said anything.'

The truth enrages me and I am screaming now.

'You said you loved me, you said you loved me once.'

He is backed up against a door now. His hands are held out to keep me at bay. His voice is calm. 'I never said that in the daylight, you know. Never.'

He is right. I stand still there, sweating and heaving and dazed but I know that he is telling me what I have known all along.

An odd look passes across your father's face. 'It was Mama who had fallen in love with you.'

I shiver at his words.

'I want you to leave the house,' my voice is as brittle as ice. 'You can decide whatever it is you decide away from here and let me know later.'

~

There is a secret place just outside Guwahati, off the highway going to Kaziranga and Jorhat and all those places beyond, that I will take you to one day, little one. It is a clearing in the woods, a still, shady place. A small creek bubbles along on one side of it and on its edges are strewn boulders, some perfect for sitting on.

Joya and Bidyut used to go there often; then Ron and I went, once, when I insisted.

Ron was bored; the odd hush alarmed him, he imagined snakes under every boulder or rotten tree branch. I had been entranced by the small, shallow stream: it was so clear I could see right down to the bed littered with round stones and weeds. Tadpoles flickered around the edge of the water. Ron was disgusted but I—I wished I could lie down on the water and float away to all the magical places the brook travelled to.

When Joya died, I took to my bed and as I lay there, looking up at the featureless ceiling, I imagined I was afloat on that stream. I submitted to it eagerly as the warm waters carried me away through that unknown jungle. As I drifted along, as light and insignificant as a dead leaf, I felt a curious sense of freedom. The blue sky played hide and seek with me through the forest canopy. The sun dazzled my eyes until all I could see were a million suns. I could have stayed there forever.

Your father retrieved me from that stream. He plunged right in and lifted me out of that healing water. He brought me to shore. He rescued me and I let him think that.

I go to that stream now. I lie in my bed and wait for the waters to call and I immerse myself in their warm embrace. Through the green tops of trees I watch the sky wheeling around. Does this make you dizzy, little one?

At night I take care not to lock my door so that Mary can enter in the mornings. She brings me breakfast in bed and I smile at her and I eat. I want to take care of you and I do not want to alarm anyone else.

'Ayya should not have gone on tour now,' Mary grumbles as she tidies the bed around me.

'He had no choice,' I calm Mary down.

'Would you like to come out, madam?' Mary asks hopefully, every morning.

'I am fine here,' I smile, 'anyway, the doctor said to take rest.'

So, along with my meals—she has taken to staying back in the evenings until I eat my dinner—she brings me the papers, the phone and the mail.

Preetha calls and we chat every day; Mama calls and I am cheerful on the phone. Ma is annoyed with Ron for travelling at this time, but I reassure her that this was the way big companies operated.

One morning, the bell rings. Mary comes in to say the lady who had come to dinner wanted to see me. Preetha?

I haul myself out of bed; I haven't bathed for two days now, I smell rank and I look about as bad. But still I walk slowly to the veranda where Mary has installed her.

From the corridor I recognize the sleek head bent over a magazine. I am dismayed. What could Sonia possibly want?

'Hello, Kaberi,' Sonia stands up as I step out on to the balcony.

I avoid her and go around the table to the other side and sit. 'Sorry,' I smooth my hair down as best I can. 'I look terrible.'

Sonia is sitting on the edge of the sofa, her joined hands between her knees that are pushed together.

There is a silence, heavy and clumsy. Then she begins.

'Kaberi, I am so sorry,' Sonia says, 'I didn't know or I wouldn't have invited her.'

'Didn't know what?' My tone is so caustic I don't recognize it.

'About Ranjit and that woman, their affair,' Sonia shifts in her seat.

I am silent. I do not believe her.

She drops her gaze.

'I know you probably do not believe me, but that is the truth,' Sonia's voice is even.

She continues in that same level tone. She is now sitting back in the chair, legs crossed at the knees. 'I found out that same night,' she said.

'How did you find out?'

'Rahul told me. He had to, Ranjit was frantic, looking for you, and I was right there.' Sonia pauses. 'Rahul knew, of course, he had always known. And not said a word to me.'

Slow and steady Rahul. Loyal friend.

'I came to apologize for causing you so much pain that night, inadvertently, but pain nevertheless.' Sonia looks straight at me and I get the odd sense that we are seeing each other for the first time this moment. She continues. 'Kaberi, I know you don't think much of me. We are friends only because we have been thrown together by our husbands. You will not believe this again, but I am fond of you. But I must tell you, you terrify me. You do!'

I am so shocked, I laugh. 'I? Terrify you? How?'

'You are pretty intimidating, with your deep, deep thoughts locked up behind your tranquil face.'

My thoughts are tumbling around without sense; if Sonia thought this of me, what were others thinking. What of Ron?

'I believe you, Sonia,' I say quietly.

'Thank you,' Sonia lights up a cigarette and just as quickly stubs it out in Ron's ashtray.

Mary is hovering in the doorway. 'Tea, madam?'

'Yes, Mary,' I say, 'and your chocolate cake.'

I lift my legs onto the sofa and fold them underneath me. 'Tell me about this woman, Sonia,' I say.

Sonia is puzzled. 'Don't you know about her?'

'No,' I answer. It is true—I know nothing about her at all. I haven't wanted to know about her till now, as if not knowing would make her go away.

Sonia raises her hands, pink palms up. 'You do know she works in Ranjit and Rahul's office?'

'Yes,' I reply. 'I know that.'

'Her name is Lakshmi,' Sonia begins. 'She works in the Human Resources department of the company; she has been with them about four years now.'

'What does she look like?'

'Well, not half as good as you, that is for sure,' Sonia's voice is hard. 'She is shorter than you and is plump. Fair, not so fair either, and a regular face. Very regular, nothing you would look at twice. She has very short hair cut down almost to the scalp. And yes, she wears a nose ring. Gives her a sort of Delhi University bohemian look.'

I listen with no comment.

Mary brings in the tea. Sonia helps herself to some cake; I do not feel like eating.

When Mary leaves, Sonia resumes. 'She comes across as very nice; when I first met her I remember thinking she was really too nice. Do you know what I mean?'

I nod.

'Lakshmi is always looking for someone to help. To get lunch for, to go shopping for, to help babysit someone's kids. In the office, Rahul says she is always helping others out—at the cost of her own work.'

Sonia narrows her eyes. 'And she speaks with a tongue so sweet it can only be forked.'

So, Lakshmi did not manage to seduce Sonia.

'Men adore her and, you will be surprised, women too. But I always say, someone with that much time on her hands has to be someone with no life of her own. She is like a parasite, you know, feeding off the lifeblood of someone else.'

I have this vision of a bloated bug sucking away at someone's blood.

'I am being bitchy, no?' Sonia says. 'But I can't help it, she gives me the creeps. And I was right; women who befriended her found they were inexplicably losing their friends.'

'And husbands,' I say dryly.

'Yes,' Sonia said, 'And that is what slowly swung public opinion against her. Rahul dislikes her and thinks Ranjit is behaving very badly towards you.'

I smile.

'No really, he does and I do too. And I wish I had known earlier.'

'What would you have done?' My voice is breaking now.

'Been there for you a little more. But Rahul says to say, and I am saying it too, that although it is none of our business and we cannot influence Ranjit, we are there for you. You and Baby.' She adds softly. 'Whatever you decide to do.'

Sonia moves across and sits beside me. I bury my head on her shoulder. It is hard and bony like Joya's but at this moment it is the softest place in the world.

Joya did not know how to give up. The harder and stronger and taller the wall in front of her she fought against it even harder. 'You'll break your head, one day,' I would always tell her angrily and she would screw up her face at me and say, 'So what?'

In the end, she did break her head. They blew her apart.

It was a health camp organized by the medical college; it was deep in territory controlled by the insurgents and when the circular was sent around asking for volunteers, very few put down their names. Joya's name was on top of the list.

On Saturday, the evening before she was to go, she had called me.

'Do you have to really go?' I had tried a last time.

'Hey, girl, those terrorized people there in the hills need health care as much as you do—maybe more,' she flared up.

'Okay, baba, let's not fight,' I calmed her down.

We chatted for a while and then hung up. 'Call me at night when you get back,' I reminded her.

The phone rang the next night, but it wasn't her. It was Bidyut to say the chartered bus the doctors had been travelling in had been bombed. No survivors, not one.

We mustn't give up, little one, you and I.

After Sonia leaves I switch the geyser on in my bathroom and when the water is nice and hot I wash off all the sweat and grime on my skin. From my collection of maternity clothes, I pull out a pair of denim dungarees that I had been saving for these last months and slip into it.

Mary strips the bed for me and washes the soiled sheets in the machine. She sends me out of the room and flings open all the doors and windows and sets about cleaning it.

As I sit at the computer, starting with checking my mail,

she puts a plate of chocolate cake and a fork next to it. It is delicious.

Tara is sounding desperate, poor thing. This time, child, we must finish the editing this week. I begin work, and work steadily; not all the time but a certain two to three hours, in breaks, each day. By the end of the week, we are done. Congratulations, Tara writes, and I send her a smiley in reply.

The day after I finish I call Preetha. I do something unusual, 'Are you at home, Preetha?' I ask. 'I would like to come over.'

This is the first time I am in Preetha's house. It is smaller than mine but makes mine feel cluttered. Few pieces of metal and wood furniture are placed exactly in certain spots. Preetha ushers me to the most comfortable-looking chair in the drawing room. Tarun who has been running around me in circles as I waddled into the room is sitting at my feet, colouring.

'Great to see you, Kaberi,' Preetha says from the kitchen as she brews us some green tea.

'Yes,' I say, 'I finished the book and wanted to come and see you two, that's all.'

Preetha gives us some CDs before I go; she wants you to be a 'super baby', so she pushes me to play baby Mozart and baby Beethoven to you. That is fine for her, she learnt the piano in that lofty school in Ooty but I finally know what I want.

Right at the back of the CD drawer in the entertainment unit is what I am looking for. You give me a hard time—my stomach gets in the way every time I sit down to search inside the drawer; finally I kneel down on all fours and find what I am looking for. There. Old songs of Bhupen Hazarika; a couple of Rabindra Sangeet and old sixties–seventies–eighties blues and rock and jazz. I discard the rock—too noisy for now—but I slip in Bhupen Hazarika first. Listen. Hear about love and longing and betrayals; listen to the Brahmaputra flowing and the wind whistling above him. Can you hear that beat like the drumming of the heart? That is the bihu, my love, and all around are the songs of the birds and the whispers of the hills.

There is so much to learn, my love. We will take it one day at a time.

Large chunks of free time stretch out before me. The book is done; a good part of your work has been tackled too. Inevitably, I feel a restlessness begin to stir inside me and I move to stifle it immediately.

'Mary,' I say one bright morning, 'please take a chair upstairs to the terrace.'

The rain tree that grows in front of our building grows over part of the terrace. A perfect arrangement as it is a natural awning and so much more interesting than an artificial one. I settle deep into my cushioned chair and look up at it. Scraps of blue sky gleam through the lacy green of the spread canopy. Small puffs of pink dot the branches; the blossoms are coming, another month and they will take over the green.

Birds wheel around slowly in the cloudless sky. Seemingly aimless, but I know better; little happens in nature accidentally.

Mary clatters up the staircase; she is carrying a peg table.

'Madam, I am bringing some juice for you,' she flashes a smile and goes off again.

This time she comes up slowly bringing up a tray on which is balanced a jug of lemonade and a glass.

The jug of lemonade is sweating on the outside; I am startled. The weather has turned again and I hadn't even noticed. The gusts of wind that rock the rain tree no longer have a cold edge; they are pleasantly warm on the skin. Why, soon our brief spring and then summer will be here.

Mary is standing at the edge of the terrace, leaning on the low wall that bounds it. I join her there. There is a magnificent view to be had from here—although we are only four floors up, most of Bangalore is only four floors high, a happy fallout of city building rules. One is like a bird perched up here: on my left I can see far across the hockey field to the other side of the park and in front, the coconut trees hedging the buildings right on Richmond Road. To the right, the view is crowded with buildings built close together and there is not much to see.

The park, of course, is right at my feet. At this late morning hour it lies deserted, its shrubs and flowers drinking in the sun; the coarse sand underneath the swings lies undisturbed, not forced to billow up in the air by children's feet. The fountain is shut off too and it is still. Children's voices suddenly splinter this hush. Where are they? There are none to be seen.

'Mary,' I turn to her, 'From where do these noises come?'

'From the play school on Wellington Street, madam,' she replies.

Of course, and I had never noticed before. A play school, perfect for you, little one.

I stretch in the sun like an animal after a long hibernation; my bare arms tingle in the sun as if it is newly grown skin. I have moulted, I think and I smile to myself.

Such a beautiful noise, the laughing sounds of children at play. I can almost see them jumping, whirling, falling and skipping. At school, I don't remember being so loud. The expectation was that we would be good, quiet children and I fulfilled every need that was required of me. You are going to be a noisy one, child, I will expect that of you.

A man with a pushcart is turning into our lane. I lean over to see; the wind pushes me, but with you now, I am heavier, stronger. Guavas. He is selling guavas; some ripe and yellow and some that are still green and hard.

'Oh, Mary,' I say, 'let's get some guavas.'

Mary peers over. 'Hey,' she calls out to the man pushing the cart, 'wait, will you!'

The guavas are delicious; Mary has washed them carefully and cut them into large wedges. She has arranged them on a large plate and in one corner, in a sauce bowl she had put chat masala.

'Mary,' I say as she puts the plate down, 'come join me.'

She is surprised, I can see that, but she sits down on the warm concrete beside my chair and we eat the warm wedges together. The chat masala is tangy and salty and when sprinkled on the soft pulp of the fruit it is heavenly. Like the salted lemon pickle Joya and I would steal from our mothers' kitchens; it was wedges, sometimes even a whole lemon that had been plunged into brine and then dried. It looked unappetizing, black and leathery, but when that first soft piece melted on our tongues we would shudder in delight.

Mary is sucking happily at her piece of guava; she is licking off the masala like a child. I have never seen her like this, my dignified Mary! What a fragile thing perception is.

As I watch Mary, I feel a stab of guilt; I have been so immersed in myself that I have not enquired after Anil, her son.

'Mary,' I ask, 'How is your son now?'

'Better,' she replies, 'he is taking his pills now.'

I am relieved. 'That is good,' I say, smiling at her.

The terrace is an entrancing place. It is bare, the floor only cement swept clean but the sheltering tree and the blue sky above are enough decoration.

In our Guwahati house there is an amlokhi tree in a corner of the front garden. Its feathery branches cast a cool shade on the grass below and Joya and I would drag bamboo mats and lie there with our books and packets of potato chips.

The hibiscus hedge screened us from the road and there we were, outside in the world yet away from it.

Here, on this sunny terrace, I feel that same freedom this morning: in the wide world, yet shielded from it.

At five in the evening, I am at the doctor's. She tells me all is well, but that from now on I will have to come and see her every two weeks until the delivery.

As I had known he would, your father calls late in the evening to ask after you. Then he tells me he wants to meet me, to discuss something. I tell him I am too tired right now, could he wait a few days. I have a vague feeling he has made his decision but now, this time, I had some decisions of my own to make.

n i n e

Before the next day dawns, so early it is still dark, there is a phone call.

Bipul Moha calls to say that my father died a few minutes ago. He slipped away quietly into that deep dark from where no one returns. He went as he had lived, removed from us, immersed in his own world. Bipul Moha whispers words of comfort into my ear but I am not listening; I have already begun planning my journey back to the house with the amlokhi tree.

This is not how I would have liked to take you home, little one, but what choice do I have now?

As soon as Bipul Moha hangs up, I pack a small bag silently in the dark; although there is no one to hear me in this flat I still take care to move around softly, without sound. I do not pack much: a few underclothes, a couple of salwar kameezes, a few blouses, kaftans for the night and my toiletries. I will borrow petticoats and mekhela sadors from Mama or Bina Mahi.

With the packing out of the way, I work my way methodically through the house: I turn off the gas, make sure the dustbins are emptied; I check that the balcony doors are secured well and that all the windows are bolted. The television is off but I check the main switch anyway. The house keys sit at the bottom of my handbag, a lump of cold metal, but I cup them in my hand just to feel their weight.

Then I wait. It does not take your father long to arrive; he comes prepared to leave too, with a small bag and arrangements made at the airport for two tickets to travel to Guwahati via Kolkata.

The sun rises as we take off from Bangalore. From my seat in the first row I watch it without the usual accompanying excitement. But when the plane dips and turns to land at Borjhar, nearly four hours later, I feel my stomach tighten briefly, very briefly, with excitement as I catch a glimpse of the Brahmaputra, splintered into lacy tendrils by the broad banks of sandbars it throws up in winter.

Mama is waiting by the exit gate; she waves out frantically to me as your father and I walk towards her.

She enfolds me in a hug as soon as we cross over. 'Poor darling!' she says as I rest my head on her shoulder. 'You must be feeling awful.'

I am feeling terrible; my stomach hurts; my back aches and my feet are swollen so badly I can hardly fit them into my sandals. What I do not feel is grief. I do not know what to feel for my father who had been no more than a shadow in my life. I had hoped landing in Guwahati would set off some sort of trigger and I would feel the right emotions but all I feel still is an overwhelming exhaustion and an increasing anxiety about my wholly inappropriate reaction.

Just beyond the airport there is a grove of betel nut palms; they grow tall and slim and closely ranged together and gather below them a shade that is so cool, so alluring that every time I pass by I feel a shiver down my spine. Sometimes the urge to run into that shade and hide myself in it is compelling. This morning, more than ever, I want to be left alone to lie down there and rest awhile.

We pass sights that have been made familiar by years of travelling the same road; this is the only way into town from the airport. Look carefully, child, this is where it all began. Across the grove is Mountain Shadow, the air force base, laid out in the straight lines that can only be laid out by military men; but even these are softened here by the ever moist air and the rains that pour down from the skies like a celestial waterfall. Banyan saplings grow out of cracks in the encircling walls and wild vegetation burgeons in the bits of land left untouched by man.

There is little traffic at this time of the morning and we make good speed. The road cuts through an almost rural landscape of paddy fields and clumps of tangled trees. Look, there on our right is Deepor Beel, a marsh, supposedly protected, where wild birds come to seek sanctuary. Brick kilns grow like cancerous growths along its edges choking it gradually so that one day it will surely give up and die, this wild wetland. The road now cuts across the University campus: large buildings, once grand, but now haggard and dishevelled, line the road on both sides.

'There,' Mama says, her voice light with affection, 'look, there is my old department—the English department.'

My phone rings as we approach Kamakhya; it is Preetha. I turn it off and begin to text instead. *Sorry, am in Guwahati. My father died this morning.*

Up ahead, on our left, Nilachal hill stands gravely in the morning sun; we all bow our heads in obeisance to the ancient Kamakhya temple there. As we skirt the base of the hill, my phone buzzes; Preetha has replied. *Oh God*, she writes, *I am so sorry. Let me know if you need anything*.

There are leopards on this hill, little one, really, in fact leopards roam many of the hills in our town, even today. This is a town of small blue hills and of green flatlands between these hills, but most of all, this is a town of the river that flows imperiously through it. The Brahmaputra—the Son of Brahma, the Creator—and he truly is magnificent. Fit to be descended from a God.

That first glimpse of the river is always a special one—has he changed since the last time? Is he full and arrogant or has he diminished with the cold? This morning the river is riding higher than I remembered from last time, two years ago, but that had been deep winter. It is still winter here but the cold is waning and soon, spring will swoop down on the unsuspecting town.

To our right, the squalid mass of Fancy Bazaar remains unchanged; if anything, it is filthier than I remembered. Better to look at the river, eyes averted from the market area, child. And look, there are the old steamers there, tied up—one of those must be Bidyut's restaurant!

'You must be patient, child,' Mama pats my hand with her cool, dry one. I am startled—she uses the word patient in place of brave, but I know what she means.

Into the heart of the city now: on our left on a rise the Deputy Commissioner's bungalow—I remember it had a thatched roof years ago, but now, that has been replaced by a tin one; we pass Judges Field and then turn right driving along the Long Pond. Off that peaceful length of water the driver turns into one of the small lanes. We emerge on to Lamb Road and then along the banks of another ancient pond, two actually, mirror images of each other, Jorpukhuri, the Twin Ponds, and another shortcut later the car turns into our little street along the base of Chitrachal Hill.

The car lurches to a stop outside my gate. Ron steps out of the car and the driver rushes to open Mama's door. She looks at me and pats my hand one more time. I sit in the car while the others walk up to the gate; they let me be and I grab the time granted. Through the open windows cold air comes pouring in, flushing out the warm, stale air inside. Despite the cold, I am sweating, I am so terrified I can smell the fear in my sharp sweat.

I stand under the amlokhi tree.

The feathery branches are loaded with the marble-sized green fruit; they are translucent in the morning sun, their veins prominent as if they would pop under any unaccustomed pressure. I cradle my heavy stomach in my hands, standing there awkwardly under the old tree.

Silence emanates from the house; no noise, no wailing, no clanging of pots and pans, no wheezy cough coughed by an old man. I am filled with dread again.

'Majoni.' Bina Mahi steps lightly down the cracked concrete steps that lead up to the veranda. She moves swiftly towards me, her muga mekhela crackling with every step. Her pretty face is swollen, her crimson phut smeared as if she is the bereaved wife. As she puts her arms around me I smell that familiar mixture of dampness and Cuticura talcum powder.

Shoes and sandals are piled up together in an untidy sprawl in a corner of the veranda. I step out of my sandals there; the smooth cement floor is cold under my swollen feet.

In the front room the green casement curtains have been hastily pushed aside on their rods but it is still dim; there are too many people gathered here. The small room has been emptied of all furniture and there in the centre, on a bamboo mat on the cold floor, lies my father. His body is draped with white unstitched cloth, but his face is uncovered and an oil lamp glows beside it. Incense sticks drip ashes on the floor; their perfume mingles with that of the ripe fruit heaped on botas and sorais all around the room, and my stomach heaves.

They have been waiting for me; when I enter all eyes turn towards me and I can hear an exhalation, a long susurration of relief that now the lifeless body can begin its journey into the unknown. All the glances roll off me; I can feel only the hot gaze of one pair of eyes and I turn to my right. There, at my father's feet sits my mother. She is dressed as she always is, in a white mekhela sador, but there is something incomplete about her attire. Of course. She has discarded whatever little jewellery she wore: her gold and pearl earrings and the pair of thin, twisted gold bangles she wore on each wrist.

Someone has placed a murha next to her and I lower myself, heavy and graceless, on to it. As I sit down Ma reaches for my hand and grips it hard with her rough one. She does not let go of it all morning; she clings to it as mourners come up to her to mutter their awkward condolences; she holds on harder when they lift my father to carry him out to the cremation grounds in Nabagraha.

My mother does not say a word and I am glad of it. I cannot bear to hear her say anything this morning; I will not be able to speak in return.

As the assembled mourners disperse, Ma and I continue to sit there, two rocks, seemingly impervious to the storm breaking all around.

Ma withdraws her hand; she wipes her eyes with the corner of her sador. 'How are you, Kaberi?' she asks. 'You have to be very careful these last two months.'

'I am well, Ma,' I say. 'And you?'

Ma's voice does not have its customary edge. 'What to do? I will have to carry on.'

Bina Mahi is now beside us. 'Come, Baideo,' she says,

kneeling down next to Ma, 'come, Kaberi. Come inside and rest a little.'

Ma allows herself to be led in like a child. She stumbles as if she is ill and then I remember that she has been up all night and Bipul Moha had said she has neither eaten nor drunk any water since the time my father left her.

Ma stops at the door leading into her room, their room, my father and hers, and shakes off Bina Mahi's hand. She puts her hand on the door frame to steady herself and then turns around. 'Not there,' she says. 'I will rest here, in Kaberi's room.'

My room has two narrow single beds along the two long walls. Ma sits down on one and does not protest as Bina Mahi raises her bent legs and places them on the bed. She lies down slowly as if it is painful to lower herself on to her back.

'Kaberi, child, will you eat something?' Bina Mahi cups my cheek with her soft hand. She uses 'you' in that familiar way that intimates use, not the distant 'you' that everyone else calls me these days. I put my arms around her and for the first time this day, I cry.

Mama appears beside me; she has been attending to the people who have dropped in on hearing the news.

The house is empty of men. They have all gone to the cremation grounds; it will be hours before they return. Sometimes the bodies take a long time to burn down and in winter it takes longer still.

My father has no son to light the fire that would free his soul, releasing it from the ties of this earth. 'Who is doing the mukhagni?' I ask Bina Mahi.

'Your Jorhat Uncles's son, Santanu,' she says as she hands me a steaming cup of tea.

Yes, my father's older brother's son, Santanu. He is stepping in for that son that my parents never had.

The tea makes me need the bathroom. I make my way

slowly to it; it is exactly as it was when I was a child. The old cracked pedestal sink, the commode with the cistern raised high above it, the sunken floor of the shower area scoured clean—Ma abided no dirt—but cracked and worn. It is still the only place I can be alone, little one, here I am, back in my old hiding place.

When I emerge Mama and Bina Mahi are sitting side by side on my bed discussing something. Ma is still, maybe asleep, with her right arm over her eyes.

'What is it?' I ask, as I waddle to my bed.

'No, Bina and I were just wondering if you should perhaps come stay at home with us,' Mama begins. 'You will be more comfortable and I can look after you. Besides Ron will be there.'

Bina Mahi murmurs agreement. 'I will stay here with Baideo, in any case.'

Home—that nebulous word again.

'No, I will stay here,' I say.

I lie down; my bed is hard and familiar. Can you feel it, little one? This is where I slept for years and years before I met your father. The pomegranate tree outside the window is in flower. The pretty blossoms catch the sun and flush crimson against the blue sky. The lazy dance of its slight branches in the wind nudges me into sleep.

Ron wakes me up. He is calling from Nabagraha; I look at my watch, it has been two hours and the cremation is not over still.

'Are you okay?' Ron asks. 'Have you eaten lunch?'

'No, yes . . . am okay. You know there will be no food cooked here for the next four days.'

There is a pause. 'Okay then, take care . . . and eat something.' Ron's voice is uncertain, as if he had meant to say something else but could not say it in the end.

The main house is quiet, although a few soft voices of women gathered in the front room sometimes find their way across the thin wall, and Ma still sleeps in the bed across. The curtains have been drawn against the afternoon sun and it is dim inside.

Familiar sounds make their way from the kitchen area at the back of the house. I make my way out to the long veranda that all the inner rooms open out to. From there, I can see the kitchen at the far end. I shuffle slowly towards it; as I descend the two steps that lead into the kitchen veranda Joymati sees me. She drops the kitchen towel in her hand and rushes out.

'Kaberi myna!' she is squealing with affection. She calls me 'Baby' and I smile at the thought. 'Sit, Sit.' She drags a murha out of the kitchen.

Golapi Bai follows her out. She moves with her usual gravity and stoops in front of me to give me a kiss on my upturned face. 'You had better eat something girl,' she says and leads me into the kitchen.

Mama and Bina Mahi are in the kitchen cutting up large mounds of fresh fruit. That is all the food we will eat in the next four days.

Bina Mahi sees me and calls out, 'Kaberi, Joymati has made some khicdi for you over at our place. Just wait a little—she will go get it for you.'

I am surprised. 'No, Mahi,' I protest, 'I will fast too.'

'Silly girl,' Bina Mahi throws me a look, 'married daughters are not obliged to fast and in any case, you are carrying a child now. You have to eat.'

Golapi Bai doles out a generous amount of hot khicdi on my plate. 'Eat,' she says. She was never one to say much, but she sits beside me at the rough wooden table as I eat, stroking my hand with her calloused one.

After a while, when she is sure I have eaten, she carries a plate of fruit out towards my room. She lifts the green curtain and enters. The hair stands on my head by what follows. Ma is wailing now; she is howling and crying out to all the powers that be to take her away too. Mama quickly steps to my side and hugs me to her. The sound still reaches me though; the cries are terrifying because they are so unfamiliar.

In all these years I have never heard my mother cry. Her cries strike fear into my heart; they tell me things have changed and will never be the same again.

After lunch, the house is still and expectant.

People are still dropping in but not as many as in the morning. Mama attends to them, while Ma still lies, motionless, on her bed. I would like to stay up and greet all these people who have come to share our grief but my back aches and I stretch out on my side of the room.

Ma has still not moved from her bed. I find I cannot sleep. That short nap in the morning has left me sleepless.

The quilt weighs heavy on me; I am not used to it anymore. I cannot lie here anymore, darling; come, let's sit out in the veranda.

My father's easy chair still sits in its corner. The polish on its wooden arms are worn down to the grain of the wood in places. That would have been where he laid down his arms everyday. The cane latticework that curved so beautifully to form the bottom of the chair is broken in places and the breaks have been repaired by crude plastic wicker.

There is only a murha in the opposite corner and I do not want to be uncomfortable now. I lower myself onto my father's chair. The chair is more a lounger than a chair and I find I am almost flat on my back when I finally lie back fully. From this reclining position I can see the amlokhi tree spread out lacily across the blue winter sky. Your grandfather must have watched the changing seasons from here—the hard, blue sky of summer softened by clouds, the threatening sky of the monsoon and the cold, bright one of winter. The night sky would have been almost the same all the time; the dark levels all differences.

A car turns into our lane. In the stillness of the afternoon I follow its progress down the road. It stops at our gate; I can see it now, it is a black Honda.

The door opens and then slams shut on the driver's side. A tall man disappears behind the car and then emerges again on my side. He is familiar to me this man, in the set of his wide shoulders and the long curve of his torso. When he is at the gate I know who he is. He has put on weight since the last time I saw him, but the weight sits well on him and he is still graceful as he twists to latch the gate.

Bidyut smiles as he climbs up the steps. 'When did you arrive?' he says. He waves me back when I begin to rise from the chair. 'Sit,' he says, 'I will sit on the murha.'

'About eleven-thirty this morning.' I say. 'I didn't see you here.'

'No,' Bidyut says squinting into the sun. 'I had already left for the cremation grounds to make the arrangements there.'

'Yes,' I say. I should have realized that.

'All this happened very suddenly, he hadn't been ill or anything,' Bidyut says.

'Yes.'

There are no words to say sorry in our language and Bidyut makes no attempt to say so now. But I know what he means as he talks about my father.

Bidyut waves at me in an odd gesture. 'No one told me about this—I didn't know.'

For a moment I am puzzled and then I see what he means. It is you he is talking about! I flush darkly. 'Not too many people know,' I reply.

'It's good,' he says, 'I am glad for Ranjit and you.'

'Thank you,' I am suddenly embarrassed.

Bidyut looks at the quiet front room. 'I have come too early,' he says.'

'No,' I say. 'It's fine.'

'Didn't think,' Bidyut shakes his head. 'Had a bath after the cremation and just rushed back here.'

When he talks about the cremation I want to ask him some things but I cannot. Not now.

'Are you okay?' Bidyut is looking at me. His eyes have changed; they are calm, no longer restless.

'Why? Why do you ask?'

Bidyut stands up and walks to the steps. 'Just asking, that's all,' he says.

He turns around back to me. His shadow falls over my face. 'You know the last time we met . . .'

'Yes,' I say quickly, stopping him before he can bring it up, 'yes, it was that time.' It does not take me long to cry now. I always cry easily for Joya. Bidyut squats down beside and lays a hand on my head.

He is still sitting there when your father walks up the footpath.

Ron stops at the foot of the steps.

'How are you, Bidyut?' he says.

'Hey, Ranjit,' Bidyut stands up and extends his hand. 'Not the best time, I know, to meet again.'

Ron shakes Bidyut's hand.

'By the way, congratulations,' Bidyut says.

Ron does not hesitate.

'Thanks, man,' he says. He look at me this time. 'Mama has sent some clothes for you,' he says. 'She says you will have to change before the evening.'

As I dress in front of Ma's dressing table I try not to look at the reflection of the four-poster double bed in the mirror. I focus on you instead, you are a big baby now, darling, and I have to knot the petticoat high above you to be comfortable. The black blouse barely fits me, the front flaps do not meet but I manage to fasten them together with safety pins. Mama has sent me several pairs of mekhela sadors, I pick the white one with the black border to wear this evening.

The bed looms behind me and despite my resolve, my eyes stray to it again and again. It is a beautiful bed, my mother's marriage bed. Her father had it made for her wedding—it is made of teak and the headboard and the footboard are high and old-fashioned; they are carved with images of lotuses and trailing vines. The polish has darkened with age, in places the fine carving is almost obscured but it is still lovely. A place of mystery for me this bed before but I know it well now.

I sit on the bed. It is high and hard.

The emptiness of the room startles me: it has always been this way, but I have grown accustomed to more clutter and now this austere room amazes me. My parents, your grandparents, have lived their entire lives this way. In the centre of the room, standing free on the floor, the bed dominates the small room. On the wall near the door is Ma's dressing table—it matches the bed, they are part of a set. The top of the dressing table is covered by a piece of white embroidered cloth, daisies clumped together and tied up with a blue ribbon. There is very little on her table: a small plastic vial of sendur that Ma will never need anymore, a small tray loaded with hair clips that are used to secure a bun in place, a bottle of talcum powder, Yardley it says on it, and pot of Pond's cold cream for the night. The only trace of my father is a small plastic comb with some teeth missing.

Beside the window looking out onto the side garden is an old wooden ulna, a clothes horse, on which is neatly hung a set of mekhela sador that Ma must have been wearing yesterday; here in this damp climate clothes are always hung out, to dry out the sweat, before they are put back into cupboards. An old white kurta of my father's, discoloured grey with endless washing, hangs limp beside it. The only other piece of furniture in the room is an old Godrej almirah, the metal painted unfashionably green, not like the sleek ones of today. I know it holds little, a few sets of Ma's clothes—including her wedding mekhela that her mother had woven for her on the loom, the white one with the diamond burfi pattern— and a few trousers and bush shirts that my father had owned.

There is an unexpected peace in this room today. Maybe because no one has thought to enter it, or perhaps people are afraid to, it is the room of the dead person after all, but I feel a measure of equilibrium I have not felt these past few hours. I remember now that I have to send news to Mary—she would have come home and would be distraught not to find me there. I should also call Sonia.

My handbag had been put away inside Ma's dresser, my phone is there. As I bend down to get it out, I catch a glimpse of my face. There is something incomplete about it. I straighten out and open Ma's small pot of sendur. With a little ivory stick kept near it I draw a small line on the parting of my hair. Ma also has a small pad of red phuts next to the sendur; I pull out one and stick it carefully on my forehead.

Mary does not have a phone; I call Vincent instead and ask him to inform Mary. I tell him I will call again when I am ready to come back.

Sonia has been waiting to hear from me. 'I did not want to disturb you,' she says. 'But let me know if I can do anything . . . anything at all.'

An afterthought, I ring Dr Joseph—she is taken aback by the news. As she expresses her regret I can hear the note of worry underscoring her words.

A steady stream of visitors begin to trickle in by late afternoon.

The first person to arrive is Bipul Moha. I am sitting on the side veranda that our bedrooms open out on to when I see him walking across from their garden into ours; he uses the small path that cuts across the hibiscus hedge, the one our two families use to visit each other. He walks with a stoop and he moves slowly, like an old man, his hands clasped behind his back. My heart contracts with concern; I hope it is only the loss of my father that has caused him to wilt like this.

He looks up at this moment and sees me sitting there, watching him. Bipul Moha straightens up and throws up his arms in a welcoming gesture. 'There you are!' he says. 'My golden one has come home.'

I walk down towards him. We meet on the grass near the gardenia bush; he hugs me to him, fiercely, and he lays his white head on my shoulder and weeps in great juddering gasps. 'Another one gone, Majoni, I cannot bear it anymore.'

The roles are reversed for the first time. This giant-hearted man who has healed my every hurt is now seeking comfort from me and I hold his shaggy head in my hands and soothe him as best I can.

I lead Bipul Moha to the rickety cane sofa where I had been sitting. He holds my hand as we talk.

'This grandchild is all I have to look forward to now, girl,' he says.

'Hush,' I say. 'We will have lots of things to look forward to from now on.'

Mama, Ron and Papa arrive soon after; Papa hugs me, he holds me gingerly as if he is afraid I may break. Mama plants a wet kiss on me as Ron looks on. I am glad he and I are separated by the tide of people swelling around us.

Ma stays in bed so I have to circulate, greeting people I haven't seen for years, decades sometimes; they all kiss me and express regret. I accept their affection easily, I am still not hurt enough to need it all.

As the sun goes down and the first stars begin to wink in the night sky, my mother sends for me.

'Sit beside me,' she says holding onto my hand. 'Don't leave me here.'

The rhythm of a house in mourning allows no time for grieving.

My poor mother lies prostrate on her lonely bed while all around her people come in and go from early morning until late at night. While he was alive I have never seen my father receive so many people, our house seldom had visitors but now it is as if everyone from the topmost bit of Upper Assam to the bottom of Lower Assam have decided to call in on us and show solidarity. My solitary life in Bangalore is almost unreal in comparison now; I do not know which the truth is.

The kitchen bubbles and simmers with this unaccustomed activity—endless cups of tea are sent out from it, steam rising from them in the cold winter air, and plates of fresh cut fruits and milk sweets are handed around. You know, little one, if you didn't know better you could almost mistake this gathering for a festive one.

After the first few days, the edge has been taken off most people's grief; barring Ma's, of course, and Bipul Moha and Bina Mahi's. Many of the visitors are cheerful, most of them are delighted to see me big with you and, darling, you have been the centre of a lot of attention.

Although I did not expect it, many of my schoolmates and college friends have dropped by; they come with children, many with two, some even with three children, and they tease me about your late arrival. Well, better late than never, I tell them and sweetheart, how fervently I believe in that, only you know.

I invite them all to the prayer meeting we plan to host on the tenth day; my father had asked that no funeral be held, no puja be done—all he wanted was a prayer to mark his passing.

As the day of the gathering draws close Ma grows agitated. She has risen from her bed and although she still does not want to go out and receive people in the front room she has fallen into her old meticulous routine. I see her stumbling from her bed in that lightening dark just before the sun rises; she makes her way, hands outstretched to prevent falls, to the bathroom attached to her bedroom. I hear her bathing, the sounds of the water and her movements amplified in that still hour. She is dressed, ready to face the day by the time the sun rises. She seems calm but I hear her tossing in bed at night; she sleeps little and I wonder at her physical resilience in the day.

The night before the prayer meeting I hear Ma tossing and turning in her bed. She is an indistinct figure under the mosquito net but the night is bright, a full moon is smiling down at us from the sky, and when the silver light catches her face I can see the worry lines carved deep in it.

'Are you awake, Kaberi?' Ma calls out after what seems like hours of fretting.

I roll over to see her better through the mesh of my mosquito net. 'Yes, Ma, I am,' I reply.

'Come here, will you?' her voice is frail.

I sit up in bed and pull out the tucked-in ends of the net from under the mattress. I cross the room on my bare feet.

'What is it?' I whisper, although there is no one to hear us.

My mother hesitates. 'Sit, sit awhile beside me,' she says finally.

I drag the cane chair in the corner near her bed and sit down beside my mother. I wait for her to speak.

Ma is lying on her side now, looking at me through the nylon netting. 'You probably think your father was a bad man, don't you?' she says suddenly.

I am caught by surprise.

'Why would I think that?'

'Because he drank and all that. Because he wasn't much of a father to you.'

'No,' I answer, 'I do not think he was a bad man.'

'Still,' Ma persists, 'you must think badly of him.'

'No, Ma,' I say wearily and that was the truth. I did not think badly of him, I just did not think of him very much at all.

'Don't you judge him,' Ma says, her voice fierce. 'He did not drink for fun, you know, he drank because he had problems.'

All men who drank would say that, I think.

Ma continues her voice urgent now. 'You know how poor your father's family was, don't you? You know how his father died when he was still in college doing his bachelor's degree, and you know how that good-for-nothing elder brother of his would do nothing to support the family. An old mother and three sisters to marry off.'

'I know, Ma,' I speak softly now.

Ma's voice is shaking with emotion now. 'He was a brilliant student your father was, people say he should have gone on to higher studies, done research maybe. But there they were, this needy family, and your father had to find a job, any job, that would feed them. He got this job in Collegiate School and took it.'

I look out at the moon. So cool and indifferent it is.

'Then there were other things . . .' Ma says.

'What other things?'

Ma's voice is hoarse with tears now. 'Your father had wanted to marry someone else. But she was of another religion and the family would not let him and found me instead.'

The room is whirling around me now. 'Did he love you, Ma?'

'What is love, Kaberi? He looked after me, in a way, and gave me respect in public.'

My voice startles even me. It is hard, cruel almost. 'Did he hit you?'

'What did you say?' Ma's voice is shaking with anger now. 'Do you realize what you are asking?'

I repeat my words. 'Well, did he hit you?'

'No! And I will say it a thousand times, no!'

I am trembling too now. 'What were the noises then, Ma? The noises late at night from across this door?'

Ma is sitting up now, knees drawn up to her. She looks directly at me. 'He would throw things, break things, you know, you heard, shout and yell.' She covers her eyes with her hands. 'He never hit me.' She drops her hand, I can see her eyes glittering with tears.

There is a pause 'But Kaberi, I always felt . . . he could have.'

I move to rise from the chair. I want to go to her, but Ma stops me with a raised hand. She is in command now. 'Go to sleep, Kaberi, tomorrow is an important day.'

The prayer meeting starts at eleven. Guests spill out from the front room into my room and out on to the two verandas.

Ma sits in the front room wreathed in incense smoke; Bina Mahi and Bipul Moha are near her but I sit outside, with Mama. We sit on the cane sofa in the side veranda; I am too big now to sit comfortably anywhere else. Also I find the incense smoke in the small room overpowering.

A male voice recites something, a passage from some text, in a monotone; the words are not clear but the inflectionless drone reaches us.

'What is he reading?' I ask Mama.

'From the Bhagvad Geeta,' Mama pats my hand absently.

They say all this chanting is good for a baby in the womb. Listen carefully, little one, absorb some wisdom.

I lean back against the tattered wicker of the chair. There is an ache in my back that I just cannot seem to shake off these days. I shift but no position brings any relief.

'Is your back hurting?' Mama twists towards me. 'Come lean against me.'

I lie back against her and she slips her hand in, at the small of my back, and lightly rubs. The warm pressure feels good. How does she do it? Mama has an enormous capacity for generosity. I would like you to inherit that from her. Ah, child, if I could I would collect good qualities from all your ancestors for you: Mama's big heart, Ma's determination, your father's application, Papa's sense of humour and . . . and what of your Koka? My father? What can I salvage from him for you?

Mama's massage and the murmuring from the front room nudge me into an odd trance-like state. I can see and hear and feel but I am as if asleep. I put my head down in Mama's lap and watch a kite fly the thermals. It wheels round and round, infinitely slowly, down it comes and again down but when I think it is about to head down into a dive it cannot possibly pull out of, it lifts its wings and thrusts up in a powerful push and heads into the blue beyond.

Ma's words of the night before come back to me; disembodied words, they seem unreal now as if they had never been said. Did I mishear Ma? Or did I misunderstand what she said? If what she said was true—and Ma never lied—Ma had lived in the shadow of violence all her life, yet today she was offering prayers for the soul of that same individual who had kept her in that darkness.

The sky is blotted out suddenly; I see before me a white shirt tucked into a pair of jeans. I twist my neck up to see; it is Bidyut.

'Hello, Jethaideo,' he greets Mama and sits down on the top of the steps leading down into the garden.

Mama's voice is warm; she has always had a soft corner for Bidyut. 'How are you Bidyut? I have to tell you, I absolutely love your restaurant!'

Bidyut smiles. 'I am so glad,' he says. He looks at me. 'How are you doing, Kaberi?'

'Not too bad,' I straighten up and sit back.

'Bidyut, I hear you have built yourself a lovely house on the hill across from us,' Mama settles her sador across her bosom.

'Where did you hear that?' Bidyut laughs.

'Bina was talking of it the other day, she says the view of the river is the best she has ever seen.'

'That's true,' Bidyut concedes, 'it is a spectacular view.'

I am lost. 'I didn't know you had built a house,' I sound petulant and I am angry. I did not mean it to come out that way.

Bidyut shrugs.

'Come and see it one day before you leave.'

'Thanks.' I stand up now. 'Would you all mind if I went to lie down?'

From my bed I listen to the chanting in the next room; it is only across a thin reed wall.

I close my eyes and imagine my father's soul rising up in the sky like a kite. Wheeling its way into the unknown.

'Why did you keep quiet?' I ask my mother at night.

'Who was there to tell?' my mother retorts.

I am seething with a rage I cannot understand. 'Me! How about me?'

'You? How could I? You were a child and moreover our child. I could not complain about your own father to you.'

'You could have told Bina Mahi? Did you? Does she know?'

My mother's voice is hard now. 'Kaberi, we are from a different time, remember. Some things are not spoken of outside the family.' She pauses. 'Besides what good would talking about it do.'

I was not going to let her off. 'Why didn't you leave?'

'And go where?' my mother is sarcastic.

I have no answer. Her own parents were dead, had been dead for a long time, and her brother would have been burdened with added responsibility.

In an uncharacteristic swing of emotion Ma begins to cry now softly.

'What is it, Ma?' I say, more gently now.

'I thought it was my fault! I thought he drank because of me, because he was tied to me for all his life when he would rather be somewhere else.'

My poor mother. 'No, Ma,' I say, 'It is not your fault. Besides they say nowadays drinking is a disease, like diabetes or high blood pressure. It is there in the blood.'

What I don't say—and she knows it—is that there are triggers that set off this disease. Was Ma my father's trigger? I look down at my big stomach, at you.

'Do you know,' I say quietly now, 'that I always thought you both were unhappy with me, because of me, that all the unhappiness in this family was because of me?'

Ma clutches at my hand. 'Oh no! Oh no, child! He loved you, your father loved you so much I was afraid for you.' She pauses. 'I told him to step back; I told him so much love would ruin you, children needed to be disciplined but he adored you. Wouldn't let you out of his sight.'

The sky trembles above us. The stars shiver.

'What?' I say, my voice shakes. 'What did you say? Ma, what did you do?'

Ma's hand shakes violently. 'Was I wrong, child? Was I wrong?'

I wrench my hand away. The tears are hot; they are scalding. 'Yes, Ma,' I whisper, 'you were wrong.'

I leave my mother sitting there on the cold veranda. I stumble down the steps and make my way down the rough path that leads to Joya's house.

If Bina Mahi is surprised she does not say so. She makes up a bed in the spare room and lies down there beside me.

Twelve square asbestos sheets painted white make up the ceiling of Joya's spare room. So many nights we lay here talking till the early morning light; and I would count and recount these same squares.

'Did you tell Joya you loved her?' I ask Bina Mahi. I know

the answer but I want to talk about love. She is lying on her side, her soft, round face cradled on her hand.

'All the time, Kaberi, all the time,' her voice is soft with love now.

There is no precise way to say love in our tongue: we say different things to express this complex feeling. I remember Bina Mahi constantly telling Joya that she was the light of their lives, their golden girl, their little darling.

'And you know Joya, don't you, Kaberi? She would be so exasperated!'

I laugh. Joya would only be irritated with all this sentiment.

'We told you too, do you remember?' Bina Mahi strokes my hair.

I did, I still do. Mahi and Moha would cuddle me and kiss me and say I was a golden girl too. I remember being confused— a golden girl and not so golden one at the same time?

'Kaberi, this house is a desert without Joya.'

'I know,' I close my eyes.

'Now that you are here, beside me tonight, it feels as if life is returning to it.'

I lace my fingers through Bina Mahi's slim ones.

She laughs but there is a break in the laugh.

'Why don't you move back, Kaberi? Give us all the pleasure of your company and of this little one?' She laughs again. 'Look at me, how selfish I have become in my old age! Your place is there now, with your husband, not here!'

I shift awkwardly.

'Are you uncomfortable, girl?' Bina Mahi raises herself on one elbow.

'Just cannot seem to find a good position these days.' I am embarrassed.

'It is exactly like that in the last few weeks,' Bina Mahi strokes my arm. 'I remember all I wanted was to get this thing out of me—sitting, sleeping, standing, there was no relief until it was out. And yet . . . when it is out, what an empty feeling!'

I contemplate my place after Mahi falls asleep. I find I do not have a place at all except with you, my little one. I consider love and all I know tonight is that I have been cheated; my own mother has robbed me of love, a love that rightfully belonged to me. And my father—I cannot think of him at all now. Cannot bear to.

I am going to tell you every day, as long as I live, and even after I die, from that great darkness—or maybe it is light—that I love you, my child. You can never love too much. Or say it enough.

When I wake up in the morning, Bina Mahi is gone. It is early still, a watery sunlight falls against the closed window panes.

From deep within the house morning sounds make their way to me. The kettle hissing on the gas fire; Bina Mahi's musical laugh as she chats with Bipul Moha. He will be reading the newspaper; I imagine I can hear it crackling.

A fish vendor makes his way slowly down our lane. Used to be, in the old days, the vendors would arrive late, almost mid-morning, and be soundly berated by impatient housewives but now all the Asomiya vendors had vanished. They have been replaced by those very aliens we had fought against, except they are called new Asomiya now. This one is crying out intermittently—fish, fresh fish—and I can hear Bipul Moha's chair being pushed back. He will be at the gate soon waiting to appraise the morning's catch.

A phone rings. Bina Mahi appears at the door, mobile phone in hand. 'It is Jeuti, your mother-in-law,' she wipes the phone with her sador.

Mama wants me to spend the day with them at their house; now that the prayer meeting is over it should be all right if I visited, she says, and anyway, Ron was leaving the next morning for Bangalore.

'I will come, Mama,' I reassure her.

'No need for you to eat vegetarian any more, the child needs nourishment,' Bina Mahi says as I step into the kitchen.

'That's right,' Bipul Moha says as he kisses me. 'We now need to look after this grandchild of mine.'

A delicious smell fills the room. Can you smell it, darling? Two loaves of warm Hussain Brothers' bread sit on the table. Bipul Moha must have driven to the bakery to fetch it straight from the oven. He stands over the table now and cuts it into thick slices. I am a child once again. Joya and I would wait every evening impatiently for the Hussain Brothers' delivery man; at the tring-tring of his cycle bell we would rush to the gate, fighting for the chance to carry the still warm loaf of bread inside.

'There,' he says, 'and your Mahi has some of your favourite jelly—look, home-made guava jelly. Eat well now.'

Bina Mahi is whipping up an omelette at the fire; she brings it hot to me. Thick and luscious, stuffed with onions and tomatoes and slathered with mustard oil.

Ma is sitting in the veranda as I make my way across the crab grass to the house. Has she not slept all night? Has she been sitting here waiting for me to return? Then I see that she has bathed and changed but there are new lines of worry on her forehead.

A spark of anger flickers inside me but I tamp it down. Meaningless now to create new rifts; better to try and let go. But I will remember, if only to know what not to do, child, with you.

'Still angry with me, girl?' Ma's voice is filled with an unaccustomed softness.

'No, Ma,' I say, 'not any more.'

I turn at the door of my room to tell her I would be going to Mama's to spend the day.

I have your first gift spread out here, in front of me. The view from the back veranda in your father's parents' house is simply glorious. I cannot describe it but in clichéd words, words can never be enough for this stretch of earth and water and sky in front of me.

The house is an old one, built by Ron's grandfather, your great-grandfather, in the early fifties; it is built on a hill on the river; it has airy, high-ceilinged rooms and gleaming floors of pink mosaic. Along the rear of the house, the side that faces the river, are wide verandas that wrap around the house at all three levels. Although every point on these open areas faces the river, the view is different because of the changes in angle. From the left corner more of the forested hillside can be seen and on the far right, the hill across the valley—the one I presume Bidyut has built on—intrudes.

But from the middle, when one stands leaning on the railing, the view is exactly centred. At the top of the picture, the sky— ever changing with every season—hangs over the line of hills that border the river. In the middle of the frame is the Brahmaputra; wide and strong and constantly moving it seizes one with its surging energy. It is impossible to tear one's eyes away from it. In the foreground, the lower reaches of the hill we stand on fall gently away to the river bank. Through the thick vegetation covering it, patches of silver sand are visible. Your own private beach, little one, we can build castles there with the damp sand while the river of my dreams flows past us.

Mama has laid out lunch on the top veranda. Steaming

joha rice and dail followed by country chicken curry, flavoured with black pepper, and rou fish tenga. A breeze blows in carrying with it the smells of the river; a damp smell but not unpleasant. From somewhere in the thick forest on our left a kuli bird calls; its sweetly plaintive cry rouses strange yearnings in me.

'Lovely to have you home, Kaberi, at last,' Mama smiles as she spoons more chicken onto my plate.

Papa breaks in. 'Cannot wait for the little fellow to arrive!'

'Hush,' Mama scolds, 'how do you know it is a fellow, anyway?'

'I don't,' Papa sucks at a chicken bone. 'I am hoping, that's all.'

'Well,' Mama sits up straight, 'we don't care what it is, really. What is important is that mother and child are well.'

She turns to me. 'Have you thought of names for the baby?'

'Ishan, if it a boy,' Ron puts his plate down.

'Splendid!' Papa wags a finger. 'Excellent! After our family deity!'

I speak carefully. 'No, we haven't discussed this at all actually. There is still time.'

Papa looks at me. There is an odd look on his face as if he is seeing me for the first time. 'What is the need for discussion? Ishan is a magnificent name.'

'How dare you?' my voice is steady, the tone mild. If anyone is listening to us they will think your father and I are discussing ordinary things. Mama and Papa have retired to their darkened bedroom upstairs and we are on the middle level now, but you can never be too sure.

Ron turns from the railing. He is framed against the afternoon sky and I have to squint at him.

'I have as much right, Kaberi,' his jaw is set in a way I know well.

All I want now is to put up my feet on a murha and slide into sleep while you listen to the sounds of the forest and the river. Yet, I know that this day Ron and I will have to enter that much avoided ring.

'What have you decided?' Ron plunges right away into the deep end.

I look blankly at him.

'Nothing.'

'What do you mean *nothing*?' Ron folds his arms across his chest.

I do not yield. 'I mean nothing. There is time still.'

Your father pushes his hands high up under his armpits. 'Not that much time, Kaberi,' he says in a thin voice.

I look beyond him at a country boat that is riding the fast current in the middle of the river; it rounds the bend and disappears from view.

'Well, I have decided, Kaberi,' Ron's voice is loud now.

I wrench my gaze away from the river.

'I am coming back home,' Ron begins, 'that is, I would like to come back if . . .'

'And Lakshmi? Are you leaving her?'

'Yes,' Ron's voice does not waver. 'I am. Will you have me back?'

There is a hollowness in my bones. Can you feel it, darling?

'Did you love me, Ron?'

Your father looks away into the forest.

'In the beginning, then later . . . ever . . . did you love me, Ron?'

He looks me in the eye. 'There are more important things than love, Kaberi.'

'No, Ron.' There is a lump in my throat. 'There are few things more important than love.'

A bulbul hops onto the railing near the mango tree. This one is also a cheeky one like my fellow in Bangalore but it does not make me smile today.

I rise from my chair. 'I will call you in Bangalore, Ron,' I tell your father.

'So, is it a no, then?'

I shake my head. 'I don't know now, Ron. I haven't thought it through.'

Everything had changed. All the fixed points on the map of my world have shifted now. Was it love that I had felt for your father all these years or did I love him merely because I had been expected to?

That night I lie awake listening to the wind in the nahor tree. The rustling of its stiff leaves reminds me of the crackling of the stiff new muga mekhelas I wore frequently, soon after I was married.

'You don't have to wear them,' Mama would say gently.

But I wished to wear them; I wanted more than anything else to do the right thing, not to do anything that would let down my parents. Ma and Deuta had brought me up well and I was not going to set a foot wrong.

'Looks silly,' Ron said one day as I was slipping out of the stiff mekhela, stained dark at the waist where I sweated faintly, even in the winter cold.

There had been very few times—so humiliatingly few that I shrank from counting them—that Ron had remarked favourably on my appearance. In my inexperience I thought that was the way it was between husband and wife. That love was so strong it did not need words to fortify it.

I should have forced Ron to talk. Maybe, then, I would have had a chance to know him. Really know him instead of this apparition I had conjured up out of my own imaginings. Yes, I think I know him a little now; but I am not prepared, at all, for what I see.

e l e v e n

T he last few days in Guwahati.

Without reason an overwhelming sense of urgency seizes me; I do not want to squander away the little time I have left. But what is it that I wish to do? I cannot name it, I cannot put a shape to it, but there is something that is nagging at me.

In the tranquil mornings, sitting in the front veranda with Ma, I am anything but tranquil. Joya used to be like this— itching, fretting, always wanting to do something, be somewhere else from where she was and I would watch her with rising exasperation. After she entered medical college she discovered a name for this—akathisia, a feeling of unrelenting restlessness. It is as if you are gripped by a disquiet so intense it is terrifying. Of course, what she described was pathological, an illness, often a result of medication but I understand, for the first time, what she meant.

Ma has taken to shadowing me; whenever I turn around, look over my shoulder or look up from my seat she is there. She waits for me to notice her and then she strikes up a conversation. She talks of things she has never spoken of before: she tells me of her childhood growing up in Shillong and when she speaks her face softens. I am unsettled by her talk; with her outpourings she is subverting the relationship we have always shared, the formal one of parent and child. I am not certain I desire this shift, sometimes I find I would like that old distance between us.

One morning as I sit in the front veranda watching the occasional passer-by she calls out to me from inside.

'Kaberi, come and see this,' her voice is tinged with excitement.

When I enter my room trying to focus in the dim light I see she is sitting on the bed. She has spread out around her old photograph albums, the kind in which black-and-white photographs are held in at corners by triangular tabs. Golapi Bai is sitting on the floor flipping through the pages of some of them; she has more time now that the household has reverted to its old slow pace.

I sit down by Ma's side. 'What are these?'

'All our old pictures,' Ma hands me one. 'Ones of your father's family when he was young. Look there are some of my sister and brother, and here, see, there are your baby photos!'

I am drawn in now; some of these pictures are ones I have never seen before and the others, the ones I have seen, have completely faded from my memory. We were not a family that sat down together on cosy evenings to pore over our family pictures. Remind me, sweetie, to take thousands of photos of you that we can look over from time to time.

There—there is your grandfather, so young, so innocent; he is wearing trousers hitched up high upon his waist, in the style of the day, the broad bottoms turned up unevenly. He is standing in a garden—in Jorhat, in his father's house, Ma tells me—against a scraggly hedge. He must be no more than seventeen. The sun is on his face and he has his face lowered, as if he is shy, and there is a lopsided smile on his untouched face. He would have had no inkling of the clouds that would shadow his life later. My father. Deuta. I run the tip of my index finger lightly over the face in the photo. I think I would have liked to have known him then. Before his life took on the darkness that I have always known.

Look, little one, there is your grandmother in a frock! She is standing under a pine tree, bare feet pushed against its rough bark and she has her hair in two long plaits on either side of her round smiling face.

'In our garden, in Laban,' Ma explains, her voice laughing.

I would never have been able to link these two faces together if they had been handed to me out of context.

Golapi Bai exclaims loudly. 'Baideo, is that you? You look so sweet!'

'Dhet! Silly girl!' Ma is smiling now.

I turn a page and there I am. Plump, with layers of chin, straight hair, the fringe framing a face consumed by enormous eyes.

'You were ten months in that picture,' Ma says leaning over the page.

Joymati tugs at the page and I hand the album to her.

'I wonder what Baby will look like,' Ma suddenly says.

I am startled. She has not asked after you too much and I did not expect her to, what with so much happening around the house.

'Like Kaberi, of course,' Golapi Bai pipes up.

'I have not really thought about it,' I say.

'No, I am just wondering, that's all,' Ma's voice has a note of wistfulness.

My surprise deepens.

Ma goes on. 'Do you know, I love babies.'

'That is true,' Golapi Bai corroborates, 'Baideo adores them.'

I sit up straight and pat Ma's hand. 'I tell you what,' I say, 'why don't you come down to Bangalore for the delivery. Golapi Bai, you too.'

Ma does not speak. She then wipes her eyes with the end of her sador. 'I thought Jeuti was going for that.'

'Yes, but you come too. I could use the help.'

The creak of the garden gate opening and shutting outside and then a voice, a man, calls out. 'Anybody home?'

Golapi Bai rises in a swift motion. 'Coming!'

She returns soon with a smile on her face. 'It is Bidyutda.'

'Is that so?' Ma struggles to the edge of the bed and tidies her sador. 'Come, Kaberi.'

Ma is smiling as she chides Bidyut. 'How did you remember us this morning, Bidyut?'

'You are always in my thoughts, Jethai,' Bidyut teases. 'Actually, I had to bring Deuta some papers he wanted and thought I would drop in here and see how you were and if you needed anything.'

'Nice of you, son,' Ma lays a hand on Bidyut's shoulder as she passes him on the way to the murha, 'keep coming, now I will be all alone.'

'We are still here, Jethai,' Bidyut sits down on the step, 'and if you ever need anything call me. Do you have a mobile phone, Jethai?'

Ma laughs. 'Me? Of course, not!'

'Well, you should,' Bidyut is serious. 'I will get you one.'

I jump in here. 'That's okay, I can get her one.'

'I know, you can,' Bidyut's voice is even. 'But I would like to get Jethai one, if you have no objections.'

'Hey, you two, enough now, stop it,' Ma is smiling.

I can see that Bidyut has not lost any of his charm. In the glow of his attention even Golapi Bai is sparkling.

'How is your business these days, Bidyut?' Ma pops a paan into her mouth. 'I hear your floating restaurant is doing very well.'

'Not bad,' Bidyut says. 'After some time, you must come and see it.' He turns to me. 'Kaberi, you must come and see it before you go, come for a meal.'

'I would love to,' I say.

Ma chews thoughtfully. 'Bidyut, now you are doing so well. What was wrong with you all these years?'

Bidyut looks down at the cracked concrete floor.

'What can I say, Jethai? Those traitors broke my spirit. And Joya's passing. That broke my heart.'

'Which traitors? Do you mean our boys?'

'Yes, Jethai, who else? The ones you and I fought for, the ones we elected to the state government! Once safely settled in Dispur they forgot all about the land and the people and what we were fighting for.'

Ma sighed. 'They let us all down, son. They let us all down. Now, the country is in the hands of those we had sought to expel.'

Golapi Bai broke in.

'Tea, Baideo?'

Ma looked at Bidyut. 'Why don't you stay for lunch, Bidyut?'

'No, Jethai, I have to meet someone soon,' Bidyut glanced at his watch. 'Some tea would be fine.'

While the others were talking I have been looking at the amlokhi tree. In the bright winter sunlight the tree sparkles. The branches are heavy with the plump green berries. All of a sudden, my tongue tingles. I have not had the time or the luxury to develop any food cravings but I am beside myself now.

'Bidyut,' I call out. 'Will you do me a favour? Get me some amlokhi will you?'

Ma clucks in alarm. 'Are you crazy, girl?'

Bidyut smiles slowly. 'With pleasure, madam.'

Very slowly he takes off his shoes and socks. Then he slips out of the jacket he is wearing and walks barefoot across the grass. Deftly, he ascends the tree until he is near a branch heavy with fruit.

'Oi Golapi, bring a large piece of cloth.'

Golapi Bai rushes in and fetches an old bedsheet. She signals to me and we walk out to the old tree. She holds one end, and I the other. Bidyut drops the fat, juicy fruit onto the cloth.

Ma watches stupefied as Joymati washes the fruit and brings it out to us with salt and chilli powder on the side.

The glistening fruit is tart and rough on my tongue. Taste it, child, this is your first taste of desire.

That night I dream my father is beside me; I can feel his hand on my brow. He is telling me he is sorry, he is sorry that he did not follow his heart and turned away from it instead.

The touch is so real I have tears in my eyes and reach out for that beloved hand. With a shock I find it is real. Ma is kneeling on the floor beside my bed and she is stroking my hair. I can see her distorted body through the mesh but her forearm and hand, inside the mesh, is real and warm.

'What's wrong, Ma?' I heave myself up into a half-sitting position.

Ma is sniffing. Is she crying again?

'It's just that you are going away . . . so far away.'

But I have been far away for so many years now.

Ma retracts her hand. She is crying softly now.

I slide out from under the net and sit on the edge of the bed. 'Come and sit here, beside me.' I help Ma up to her feet.

Ma takes my hand and holds it in her lap. 'Are you happy, child? Are you happy there in Bangalore?'

I think that my parents have never visited me in Bangalore. Every time we invited them, Ron offering to send the tickets, they would refuse.

'What will I do there?' my father always laughed and Ma would always stand by his decision.

So little they knew of my life. Still she knows nothing, my mother, about me. I take a deep breath. There is a madness coursing in my veins tonight; I am not weighing risks anymore.

'He hits me, Ma,' I say, with absolute calm, so that it seems, in the serene night, that I have spoken these words by mistake.

The nahor tree by the fence rustles in alarm.

'What did you say?' Ma squeezes my hand.

'You heard me,' I am still composed. 'He hits me, Ron hits me.'

'Why?'

I release my hand from my mother's icy one. I shrug. 'Why does a man hit someone? He gets angry.'

'Why? What do you do?'

'Nothing, Ma,' I feel my face grow hot. 'I don't do anything. What did you do?'

The tears have dried on my mother's face. She is expressionless in the moonlight.

At last she speaks.

'You never told us, Kaberi.'

I look at her. 'You never told me either, Ma.'

'That's different. Don't be insolent.'

'What would you have done if I had told you? Would you have asked me to come back home?'

'I don't know, child, I don't know!'

'What will you do now? What do you think I should do, Ma?'

My mother pulls her sador like an armour around herself.

'Should I leave him, Ma?'

My mother answers in a whisper. 'No, no, not with the child on its way, it needs a father, his name to carry.'

I do not speak. After a while I crawl into my narrow bed again. I turn my face to the familiar whitewashed wall.

'Have you told anyone else, Kaberi, about this thing?'

'No, Ma, I haven't.'

'That's good, best that way, these are family matters.'

The darkness between our beds is an ocean tonight. You and I float on it alone.

The mornings are growing warmer every day. The sun's burgeoning heat is teasing out signs of spring; the trees and bushes are tipped with fresh green and birds call out from hiding places around the garden. You will arrive into this balmy world, child, I am grateful it will be a bright start for you.

Golapi Bai is filling old Horlicks bottles with brine and the left over amlokhis. She arranges them in the sunniest spot of the courtyard. Catching sight of me watching her from the veranda she calls out. 'Kaberi, do you want me to oil your hair for you?'

I sit on a murha in the cemented bit of the yard while Golapi Bai sits on a high chair behind me. She has melted coconut oil in a small bowl and now rubs my scalp with it. Our backs are to the sun; our shadows, squat and distorted are splashed on the ground in front of me. My muscles relax and sigh under Golapi Bai's expert hands.

When I was a child I used to play this game with myself; let me show you, little one. Listening to the other world, I used to think of it as. I close my eyes and listen. For the first few seconds nothing seems different and then the tempo of the world seems to change. I hear things that I do not hear with my eyes wide open. There!

I can hear the *tonk, tonk* of a bird far away, not anywhere near us, it comes from the woods on the hillside. I know which bird it is; Bipul Moha and I had looked it up in a bird book once—it is a coppersmith barbet, its cry like that of a coppersmith beating slowly on a sheet of copper. The steady drone of traffic on the main road percolates through the numerous houses that intervene between our lane and the big road. A woman's loud voice from one of the houses behind ours; she is berating a maid for mixing up coloured clothes with white in the laundry.

Another bird, this time the keteki, its melodious cry scratching at my heart—*o-ke-te-ki!* I smile; Ron says the bird calls out, *Pluck-more-pekoe*! But then he has grown up in a tea garden. A matter of interpretation, like many things in this world.

As soon as I open my eyes I lose all these sounds. The immediate surroundings now obscure that other world; the scrape of Golapi Bai's chair as she shifts, the television muttering in the front room, these are the sounds audible to me now.

Hide-and-seek. This is a game we never weary of even when we moult into adults and subside into old age.

The phone rings. Ma must have answered it for the ringing stops.

She appears in the doorway. 'Kaberi! Bidyut is on the line. He wants to know if you would like to go across to his house for lunch. He can pick you up in an hour.'

What time is it now? I lift my wrist—ten already!

'Okay, Ma, tell him I will be ready,' I call out.

jahnavi barua

Golapi Bai tugs at my hair. 'Another two minutes and we will be done.'

The hot water from the shower steams up the bathroom, I have to wipe the spotted mirror to see myself. These days, a stranger looks back at me in mirrors. The outline of my face is blurred, my features are thick with the extra weight. I resemble the old photo in Ma's album, double chin and all.

We are on the same road I took to go to Mama's house. But at the crossroads near the medical shop we do not turn left and instead carry on straight ahead towards the river. A warm wind blows in through the open windows; I imagine I can hear the cry of the cormorants on it. This road leads directly to the river and runs along it before turning off into the hills. Bidyut slows down now that we are at the river.

'Do you want me to stop?' he asks.

I shake my head.

'No, we can see the river from your house, right?'

'Yes,' he says, 'we can.'

Still I cannot tear my eyes away from the river. In the morning sun, it sparkles furiously, so bright it is almost painful. Occasional boats drift down it; the birds wheel lazily in the clear blue sky above it. To the north, the hills flanking the river stand blue and mysterious.

The car is ascending the hill now. I have not been here before and I am curious. A lot of construction has happened here recently. Along the twisting road little driveways appear, leading, I presume, to houses that perch high above the road, and so invisible from it. We climb higher still, the car in first gear now, and soon on my left wherever there is a break in cover I catch sight of the river. It teases me playing hide-and-seek, vanishing behind the hillside and then appearing, laughing, a few metres later.

We are almost at the summit when Bidyut turns left onto a gravel driveway. This runs between two shoulders of the hill and moreover it curves to the left up ahead, so I cannot see what lies in front. Instead, I focus on the two banks of the hill on either side of us; they are covered with ferns and touch-me-nots and small shrubs with pink blossoms that look strikingly like the rhododendron flower.

Then with a flourish the two walls of earth fall away and there before us on a narrow strip of land is the sweetest house I have seen in a long, long time. A narrow house, accommodating to the contours of the land it stands on, it presents its side to us, while behind it stretches away and turns a right angle into an L shape. The slanting roof of corrugated tin is painted green; rainwater guttering edges it neatly. The walls are dazzling white in the sunlight while the dark wood window frames and door provide relief from the glare. There is a garden all around! I can see vegetables growing in the back and flower beds in front. I ease myself out of the car; child, you are quite a weight these days.

As I step out and find my balance, I lift my eyes casually to the river front. The hair stands up on my arms. This view of the river is one I could not have imagined before.

Bidyut is at the door, he has unlocked it and is calling out to me. 'Come in, are you going to stand there all morning?'

We enter a small hallway; it is flooded with light and I can see why. On the left, on the front, the wall is a sheet of picture glass. Framed within it is another view of the river. The golden light, the dark wooden floor make this space so welcoming I feel as if someone has put his or her arms around me.

Bidyut leads me in deeper; we are now in the long living space. Again on the left large glass sliding doors look out on to the river. As Bidyut unlocks them I look around this surprising house. The floors are a dark wood—must be one of the local woods, bhola maybe—and the walls are ivory. This long room is sliced into two by a low wall to my right; the wall is topped by a slab of gleaming black granite, I guess that the bar must be on the other side of this wall. A wooden dining table, its polished top soft and lustrous, stands beyond this divider. And yet again, the wall to its right—the back wall—is glass, affording a view of the kitchen garden.

Off the dining room is the kitchen; I walk into the space and find it to be yet another light-filled cube. The woodwork is of light wood—looks like pine—and the granite counter tops gleam as the light bounces off them.

I step out bewildered. Has Bidyut really done this on his own? When did he learn to love these clean lines? How did he know to deepen the warmth of the wood with the colours of the forest? He has used dark brown everywhere as a base and then cleverly lifted it with odd splashes of rust and green and cream.

Bidyut is leaning on a door frame and watching me. 'The bedroom is that way,' he says pointing to a small alcove off the living area.

'Are you sure?' I hesitate.

'Go right in.'

Another captivating view. The bed is to the right of the door, placed against the back wall so that from it you looked out on to the sweep of the river.

Bidyut has very little furniture; in the bedroom apart from the bed and the built-in cupboards there is an old teak dresser with a mirror on top and a cane lounge chair by the picture window. Echoing this, the living–dining areas too are sparely furnished: the dining table in the back, and in the front, a sectional, L–shaped sofa; wherever you sat on it you could look out at the view.

'So you approve?' Bidyut is teasing now.

I laugh out loud. 'It is lovely.'

Stepping over the threshold I am in the veranda that fronts the living area. A cane sofa with deep cushions beckons and I sit on it.

The Brahmaputra flows right below us. Because of the steepness of the hill we are as if suspended right over it.

Not even two days have passed since I was at your father's house sitting in front of this same river but this morning the river takes me by surprise. Have I really seen it properly before? The river is so much closer today; I can see the water separating into different streams of current. Without its enclosing hills its boundaries have expanded until it feels limitless. The bend in the river as it flows downstream is clearly visible; I feel as if just beyond it will fall into the flat sea it is striving so hard to reach.

'Unbelievable, right?' Bidyut hands me a glass of juice. He gets himself a can of beer.

I nod. 'Yes, and so different from how I have known it.'

'You would have seen the river from Ranjit's house?' Bidyut stands against a pillar at the corner.

'Yes.'

'You can't see the full picture from there.'

I am curious. 'When did you build this house, Bidyut?'

Bidyut sits down on the other end of the sofa. 'You know Joya and I had bought this land soon after we were married. We did not do much with it, although we would come up here on Sundays with a picnic lunch and Joya would enjoy the view till lunch and then announce it was time to descend to the real world.'

'Totally Joya!' I laugh.

'Yes,' Bidyut smiles. 'Then I went through this dark time, I am sure you have heard all about it, and this land lay here empty.'

I make no comment about the dark time I had indeed heard a lot of.

'Two years ago Bhaity, you know my kid brother, got married. That was when I began building, the old house was full of people, my parents wouldn't mind me leaving at this point. It took a year to build and I have been here ever since.'

He changes the topic. 'How is Jethai doing? She seems okay and Jethai is as tough as they come.'

I take a sip of the sweet juice. 'I don't know, you know, Bidyut. I used to think so too, but I am not sure now.' I laugh. 'I find I worry about her these days. And I am so far away in Bangalore.'

'You seem to have buried the hatchet with her, Kaberi,' Bidyut is thoughtful.

I am startled. 'Really? Do you think so? Actually, things may be worse, I don't know.'

A large boat with a picnic party floats by us; they are headed to a sandbar that has been thrown up by the river just at the point where it curves left.

Faint cries from the boat float in on the breeze.

'I can see why you wouldn't want to live anywhere else in the world,' I set my empty glass carefully down on the table.

'Even if I didn't have this view I wouldn't live anywhere else in the world.'

I knew he wouldn't; Joya and Bidyut had a feeling for this land that I could never understand fully. I still don't, I suppose. For me home is where my people are; right now home will be where you are, my darling.

Bidyut seems to have read my mind. 'Do you think you could ever stay here, Kaberi?'

'If I had to for a good reason, I could.'

It is a relief Bidyut does not probe further.

'You know, I am so happy for you and Ron,' Bidyut suddenly says.

I don't understand and I stare at him,

'About the baby, silly girl, this is such a great thing,' Bidyut's face is sombre.

Another wave of recklessness sweeps over me; I am past the point of discretion. 'Well Bidyut, things are not so great really, Ron hits me.'

Bidyut's eyes widen for an imperceptible moment.

'What did you say?'

I repeat myself calmly. 'He pushes and shoves and beats me—when he is angry, of course, not very often, but often enough. And for some time now he has been with another woman.'

Bidyut shakes his head as if a fly is buzzing around in it.

'Why haven't you said anything?'

I am laughing suddenly. 'To whom? The police?'

'No, no, stop laughing. I am so sorry, I should have been there for you, so selfish, oh God.'

Bidyut is so distraught I find myself comforting him. 'It's okay, I can manage,' I pat his hand.

He grips my hand and before I can anticipate it, Bidyut leans over and kisses me softly on the mouth.

And then he leans over again and kisses me again. I am shaking now. Don't be afraid, little one, this will pass too.

'Joya comes to me when you are around,' Bidyut is looking down at his clenched hands.

When I speak my voice is trembling. 'I am not Joya, Bidyut, make no mistake.'

He fixes me with an odd look. 'I know that well, Kaberi, I know you just as well as Joya did.'

There is a pounding in my head. I cannot sit through lunch

now. 'Can you take me home, Bidyut?' I say. 'I don't think I am up to lunch today.'

All day long, contrary thoughts keep whirling around in my head. Did I do anything to encourage Bidyut? Something? Anything? When I close my eyes that fateful moment keeps appearing in my mind. It is wrong, all this cannot be happening. I feel unsteady as if walking on ground during an earthquake. But as I slip and slide and grope my way around, a seed of a thought grows larger in my head: when Bidyut kissed me it should have felt sinful; it should have felt inappropriate but the truth is that it did not feel anything like that at all. What it felt was natural, as if after a long time, the planets were finally moving into place. It frightens me this feeling; I could so easily lay myself down and submit to it.

Bina Mahi rings the next morning to suggest an outing, a drive to cheer us all up.

'Let's go up to Nabagraha Temple,' I suggest. I want to stand in that field Joya and I had discovered.

Bipul Moha grumbles as I direct him into the small lane branching off the main road just below the temple. The old dirt track has been asphalted now and houses crowd both sides. We drive on for considerably longer than I remembered walking up to and still we see no field. Bipul Moha backs carefully for a while, so I can look again but still no field.

Then it dawns on me. Our field, full of clover and touch-me-nots, is gone and the river has vanished too, behind rows of concrete houses that grow like cancer all over the once bare hillside.

Grumbling about this diversion Bipul Moha manages to turn the car around in someone's front yard. This time we head straight up to the temple. We step out of the car; Ma, Bina Mahi and I stroll downhill while Moha sits on a rock with a cigarette, near the car. I look up the temple, its ancient walls dark with age. What secrets did it hold? Did it really see the course all our lives would take?

We leave this morning, little one.

Bina Mahi arrived early this morning, just past seven, and she has been helping Golapi Bai with my packing. I came with just a small suitcase and now I am leaving with two big ones; they are loaded with things for you: vests, knitted sweaters, socks, blankets, swaddling cloths, soft toys, there is a mountain of things in there! Bina Mahi and Bipul Moha have raided the shops for you, even though Ma has not been able to get you anything. She promises to knit for you; she will bring the things when she comes to Bangalore in March.

In a lull in the packing Ma appears from her bedroom with an armload of old photo albums, the ones we had gone through. I am moved, this is a precious gift indeed.

By ten o'clock Mama and Papa arrive too; they have come with little, only a box of sweets for Ron and me, Mama says she will bring all the things she has gathered when she flies in.

Eleven o'clock and the cars are waiting outside. Bipul Moha insists on driving me to the airport even though Papa's car is there; Bina Mahi says she will come too.

Ma stands uncertainly on the veranda as the luggage is loaded. When did she grow so tentative? I hug her and she kisses me awkwardly on my cheek. Golapi Bai cries and puts her hard arms around me.

As I step into Bipul Moha's passenger seat in front I turn around one last time. I know I shouldn't but I cannot resist all the same. Ma stands there on the top step in her white widow's attire; Golapi Bai stands behind her, a hand on Ma's shoulder.

We drive through Ujanbazaar; it is a Sunday and the main road through the bazaar is emptied of its usual mass of people. The road then takes us past the High Court and I admire the lovely proportions of the old building. On the right, the river can now be seen intermittently, through gaps between the old bungalows; first the Chief Justice's double-storey wooden bungalow that always reminded me of a two-tiered birthday cake, then the DFO's old bungalow falling into disrepair now. Then we pass the Deputy Commissioner's court and through its parking lot I see the river, clearly now, and the small island on it, Umananda. The Deputy Commissioner's bungalow looms ahead on the right and after it we cross the Sukleswar temple. Say goodbye, little one, it will be a while before we see all this again.

The river meets us now. He will accompany us as far as Nilachal Hill and Kamakhya temple. And then after we pass Saraighat Bridge we will not see him anymore although he will be there, only a few kilometres from us, shadowing us as we make our way onwards.

We are approaching the University when Bipul Moha speaks. 'Kaberi, there is something we have to tell you, Mahi and I.'

'What?' I am not in the least prepared for any serious talk now.

Bipul Moha's fingers are white on the steering wheel. 'It is this Ron business,' he says with a grimace.

I wait. I do not betray the shock I feel at their knowing about it all.

Moha shoots me a quick look. 'Baideo told us about it. She also said she did not react quite as she should have when you told her. Naturally, I told her, she was shocked, it was not unusual, but she wanted us to say something to you.'

The car negotiates a series of rumble strips.

'Well, what she wanted us to tell you is that you are welcome to come back and stay with her; there is always a home for you in Guwahati. In fact, she wants to gift it right now to you. For you and the child.'

I cannot find the words to respond. I search for them but they slip away.

Bipul Moha smacks the wheel with flat of his hand. 'Why one! There are always two homes for you in Guwahati, you hear!'

'Yes, Majoni,' Bina Mahi's hand is on my shoulder.

If we were nearer home I would turn around and go home to my mother, but we are too far away. On our right is the betel-nut grove now; it tries to tempt me again but this time I have found shade elsewhere.

The plane lifts up like a giant bird released from its mooring; it is exultant as it soars into the blue sky. Below me, the patchwork of green fields and the lacy fan of the river recedes and soon completely vanishes from view but in my heart there is a strange singing. Can you hear it, little one? This unexpected tremor of happiness?

It is late evening when we touch down at Bangalore. The sky is still lit by a fitful light but at its edges darkness has already moved in.

I look for Vincent as the Jet Airways attendant pushes my trolley; I see Sonia instead!

'Hi!' I smile at her, 'Are you waiting for someone?'

She wraps her arms around me as far as they will go. 'Yes. For you!'

In the car she told me how your father had told her I was arriving and she asked him whether she could come along with Vincent to receive me.

'After your father's loss and all that I didn't want you arriving here alone,' Sonia explains.

I squeeze her hand. 'Thanks so much,' I say and I mean it.

The flat is all lit up when I walk in. I am startled; I had expected a cold, dark flat where I would have to turn on the lights myself but Mary has not only lit up the flat but has flowers in vases to brighten things up.

Mary rushes to me, beaming. 'How are you madam? Welcome home.' She takes my bag from my hand and ushers me into a chair.

Sonia sits down beside me. 'How is your mother coping?' she asks.

'She was badly shaken, but now she seems to be beginning to adjust,' I tell her. 'I think things will be fine.' Yes, little one, I am confident we will be fine.

Mary brings tea. As we sip it Sonia says casually, almost in an aside, 'Ron tells me you still haven't decided on your plans.'

'You mean about us?'

'Yes.'

'No, I haven't.'

Sonia looks at me over the rim of her cup.

'Well, whatever you decide I am there for you, Kaberi.'

Mary tells me she has decided she will stay the nights with me until you arrive. 'At such a time women should not be alone,' she declares. She does not ask where your father is at this critical time and I do not weave stories for her again.

Everything seems to be the same but I am reminded frequently that it is not really so. The light has changed—spring comes early to Bangalore and it has stolen in while I was away—the sunlight is hard and strong and it has transformed the world around. Instead of bleaching colours out as it should have, I find the light brings a depth to the world around me; I am startled by the vibrant shades I encounter everyday: the chrome yellow of the tabebuia blossoms, the azure sky, the scarlet bottu blazing on Mary's calm forehead.

The birds have never sung so sweetly. The kuli cooes from the mango trees in the Rao's garden, its plaintive call melodious yet so full of pathos. What does it cry for? The kutur kutur of the green barbet cheers me up; some of them have set up camp in the jackfruit tree in the corner of the next compound and they burst forth intermittently with their mating calls.

Mary bustles around the house and her good wholesome energy lifts me up so I find myself humming, singing songs I have not sung for a long time now. Do not laugh, little one, I cannot carry a tune but that does not stop me.

Preetha is away in Ooty, she will be back in a few days but Sonia visits often. She drops in late in the mornings and stays for lunch. We lie down on my bed after lunch like Joya and I used to and we talk. We speak of silly things and then sometimes we speak of things we that we have locked away in our hearts. I tell her of my father and as she wipes her eyes of tears and pats my hand she tells me of the mother she lost as a young girl. Her father was of the old school and he brought his three motherless children up with an extra measure of harshness lest they stray. 'Maybe that's why I have ended up so hard on the outside,' she says. She tells me that Rahul did not want children and although she had accepted his decision—she loved him and besides where was there to go—

sometimes she wanted to throw herself off a tall building. She laughs as she says that but I know of that place we all want to go to sometimes and I stroke her hair.

I feel strong these days. I take stock of work that remains to be done: a few clothes for me, some toys for you and my manuscript to be proofread. I should be able to do that in the next one month.

Vincent is driving me to Dr Joseph's clinic. She had messaged saying she wanted to see me. It has been a week since I have returned and I have neglected seeing her.

Yellow tabebuias are in full bloom in the city now. I marvel at this otherwise nondescript tree, with mediocre foliage, that sheds all its leaves only to be covered with golden blossoms that transforms its very character. There is so much hope in those bare branches that wait patiently for the flowers to conceal their nakedness.

Dr Joseph comes around her table as I enter her room. 'I am so sorry for your loss,' she says and takes my hand.

'Thank you,' I say.

The doctor tilts her head to one side and looks at me. There is curiosity in her face. 'You look remarkably well, Kaberi,' she says at last.

I smile.

'Come. Let's look at you.'

I stand on the scales. 'Perfect,' Dr Joseph smiles.

As she examines me she is talking. 'We have to plan for the delivery now, Kaberi,' she cautions.

'It is not very far away, another six weeks at the most.'

'What I would like to do, Kaberi, is schedule an elective

caesarean section. This baby is far too precious to risk,' she continues as she briskly flips through a desktop calendar.

'Okay,' I am fine with a section.

'Let's say around the end of March,' Dr Joseph puts the calendar back, 'I will let you know the exact date later, okay?'

'Fine,' I say, 'thank you.'

As the car pulls out of the basement, I call Preetha. She should be back by now.

'Hey!' Preetha's voice is warm. 'When did you get back?'

'Last week,' I reply. 'Want to meet for a coffee?'

'Sure,' Preetha says. 'Same place?'

This time I arrive at our coffee shop first. I choose a faux leather sofa where I can stretch out with you. Now, what do you want to eat, little one? Let's spoil ourselves these last few weeks, shall we? I order a large blueberry muffin and a pot of green tea.

Preetha arrives, her hair damp and smelling of shampoo. She plants a big kiss on my forehead. 'Sorry about your father,' she says as she pulls the strap of her shoulder bag over her head.

'Cappuccino,' she tells a waiter passing by.

She settles back into her corner and then crosses her long legs. She smiles at me. 'My God, you look resplendent! What happened to you?'

An image of a yellow tabebuia floats into my mind. Yes, resplendent.

'Let me guess,' Preetha continues. 'Ron and you have made up and everything is okay like in the movies.'

I shake my head. 'No, that's not it at all.'

'What?' Preetha is indignant. 'You mean that loser has decided not to come back after all?'

I shake my head again. My mouth is full of muffin. The blueberry is delicious and it is so good for the brain.

'He has offered to leave her and come back.'

'So where is the problem?'

'I have to think things through—decide what I want for Baby and me.'

Preetha's face hardens. 'Do you really have a choice? How will you manage financially? Who will support you?'

'That can be managed,' I answer airily.

Preetha takes a long draught of her coffee. 'Don't you think you are being just a little selfish, Kaberi?'

'Why?'

'The child deserves to have a father,' Preetha says, her voice hard. 'He deserves that name and that protection.'

Preetha's passion surprises me. I stare at her.

She drops her eyes.

Hesitantly she begins to speak. 'Kaberi, there is something I have never told anyone. Of course, lots of people knew anyway,' she says bitterly.

I wait.

'My father had another family,' she starts haltingly.

'I don't understand.'

Preetha laughs. 'It is not easy! He had another wife, well . . . woman, and two children from her. They lived in Coonoor, close enough to Ooty and far enough too.'

She continues. 'My mother found out accidentally when she went to lunch at an old friend's in Coonoor thinking my father had driven down to Coimbatore on work, and instead found him with this other woman and kids in Coonoor, shopping for provisions.'

I reach for Preetha's hand. 'I am so sorry,' I say.

Preetha pulls her hand away. 'I was eight and Vidya was seven the year my mother discovered this secret world of my father's.'

Her eyes are shining now. 'But you know what she did?

She arrived at an agreement whereby my father stayed on, nominally you understand, in our home. She always said that children need a father.'

I don't know what to say to her.

'Children need a father,' she repeats again.

Preetha's words come back to me as I sit out on the balcony in the evening with my cup of tea. I wonder idly what Joya would have said; what would she have advised me to do?

The sunbirds have nested in my fountain grass while I have been away. Mary says there are three little ones and the mother sits there brooding. The father is full of important duty now; he flies around busily, sometimes I think he looks tired. There he is now landing on an ear of purple seeds. A diligent father. Maybe Preetha is right after all.

From inside my cell phone rings.

I walk in slowly and pick it up. A surge of pleasure runs through me. It is Bidyut.

Your father drops in on a sunny morning a few days later. I am in the balcony checking the proofs of my book that Tara had sent while I was away in Guwahati. I am full of resolve; there is more than a month for you to arrive and I intend to finish with the book completely by then. Maybe even before Ma and Mama arrive.

'What's this?' he asks gesturing at the sheets piled up neatly on the coffee table.

I make no attempt to conceal the book from him this time—there is no need anymore. 'A book I have written,' I tell him.

Your father raises his eyebrows. 'A book?' he says. 'You are full of surprises.'

I smile.

'Is everything all right? What did Dr Joseph say?'

'Everything's fine,' I reassure him.

Your father smiles at me and his eyes crease in a way that makes my heart flutter but I make no response.

'I have moved out of Lakshmi's place,' he says abruptly.

This is a surprise. 'When?' I ask.

'While you were away in Guwahati. I am staying at the guest house now.'

He does not ask about my decision and while I am relieved I am also aware of crossing a line I cannot step back across.

The jacaranda outside your window begins to bloom a week later. I am sorting through the clothes in your cupboard when I notice it. A few tentative trumpet blossoms are peeping through the leaves but soon the tree will erupt in a lavender cloud.

I turn back to your clothes. They all seem to be in place; everything you need is here. I glance at your cot, covered now with a plain white bed sheet.

Back in my bedroom I feel an ache in my lower belly. I hope I have not hurt myself bending down to check through your clothes. Perhaps I am mistaken; it is only exhaustion.

As if to dispel my doubts a second pain grips my stomach later in the evening. I decide to go to the bathroom. I discard my salwar and sit on the commode. As I reach under, my fingers encounter an unexpected dampness. I look at my fingers; they are streaked with a rusty fluid. The cramp returns again. I am trembling now, but that will do no good. It is too early, love, much too dangerous for you to begin your journey now; I long to stop you but I am helpless. It has begun. More than a month early, dear God, but there is nothing to be done now.

I dress as quickly as I can and sit on my bed. The first thing I need to do is call Dr Joseph.

'Are you sure, Kaberi?' she asks.

I am definite. 'It is starting.'

A wave of despair begins to rise within me but I will not allow it to weaken us. Steady, little one, it is early but we will make it through.

I shout for Mary and give her instructions to close down the flat.

I pick up my phone and begin to make the calls I need to. I call Sonia, then Preetha; Sonia tells me to proceed to the hospital with Mary, she will set off from her house too. I call Vincent—he will be here in minutes. I call Bipul Moha and ask him to tell Ma. Then, I hesitate, but I call Mama and Papa; they say they will fly in first thing tomorrow.

In the car, before I put away my phone I make a last call.

I call Bidyut.

His voice is so clear, it is as if he is beside me. 'Is everything okay?' he asks.

'I think so,' I answer. 'It is starting now, my pains have started. I am on my way to hospital.'

A moment's hesitation. 'A little early,' Bidyut says. 'Let me know if you need me.'

I smile. 'I will,' I tell him and I hang up.

There. All done, my darling.

A pain seizes me once again and I give in to it willingly. I surrender to this pain that will release both of us.

See you soon, little one.

Acknowledgements

Many thanks to my early readers for their support and encouragement. I would like to thank my parents, Krishna and Bhaskar Barua; my husband, Anand; my cousins, Supriya Bezbaruah and Vandana Goswami; friend and fellow writer, Abhijit Bhaduri; and last but not least, my agent, Zoe Waldie, for the generous giving of their time.

Thank you, Diya, for your continued faith in my work. And many thanks to Paromita who made the making of the book such a calm and pleasant process.

I am also indebted to my readers, who with their enthusiastic support of my work help me to keep going on.

Read more in Penguin Books

NEXT DOOR
Jahnavi Barua

In eleven superbly crafted stories Jahnavi Barua takes us into the private, individual worlds of a varied cast of characters and exposes the intricate mesh of emotions so often concealed under the façade of everyday lives. Innocent desires and furtive longings, the complexity of fierce love and the terrible consequences of its betrayal, simple aspirations that compel brave action, life's startling reversals that reveal deep insecurities and yet pave the way for forgiveness and reconciliation—these are just some of the themes played out in these remarkably nuanced snapshots of life. Predominantly set in the verdant, politically charged landscape of Assam, yet constantly transcending the particular, the stories in *Next Door* are unerringly human. Subtle and evocative in their telling, they mark the introduction of a highly accomplished voice.

Penguin Random House India
Fiction
Rs 299